Shatter Proof

A Sonia Amon, MD Medical Thriller
By
Judith Lucci

Also by Judith Lucci

Alexandra Destephano Novels

Chaos at Crescent City Medical Center
The Imposter
Viral Intent: Terror in New Orleans
Toxic New Year: The Day That Wouldn't End
Evil: Finding St. Germaine
Run for Your Life

Michaela McPherson Novels

The Case of Dr. Dude
The Case of the Dead Dowager
The Case of the Man Overboard
The Case of the Very Dead Lawyer
The Case of the Missing Parts

Artsy Chicks Mysteries

The Most Wonderful Crime of the Year
The Most Awfullest Crime of the Year
The Most Glittery Crime of the Year
The Most Slippery Crime of the Year

Other Books

Ebola: What You Must Know to Stay Safe
Meandering, Musing & Inspiration for the Soul
Beach Traffic: The Ocean Can be Deadly!

Coming Soon from Sonia Amon Medical Thrillers

Delusion Proof
Deception Proof
Bullet Proof

Bluestone Valley Publishing
Harrisonburg, Virginia

Prologue

I jumped from my bed and crouched on the floor my arms folded around my head like fragile armor. My eyes frantically searched the dark for my enemy. Finally, I saw it. I saw the apparition of the monster! His cruel eyes shone black with hate. I waited, my breath ragged. The noise echoed in my room. My body quivered with fear and anticipation. Terror consumed my soul and panic shot through my body as I waited for it to begin. My heart thudded against my ribcage, my lungs burned from not breathing and I placed my hand on my chest to keep my heart from exploding. I didn't want to be discovered. I was terrified I would be. I closed my eyes in terror

A sharp noise - the slap! The reverberating smack echoed in the room. My face dug into the floor as I tried to escape the sound of my enemy. My mind emptied of all conscious thought as my sympathetic nervous system took over and readied me for action.

A second blow and a cry of pain. I heard bones crack. I shook like a leaf. A thousand eyes watched me. They observed my every move. I was frightened; as frightened and panicked as I'd been years ago when I was three years old. That slap and the cracked bones shattered my life forever over thirty years ago.

I felt a wisp of air pass as a large hand sliced through the air and separated the molecules. Another slap! I heard the bones crack. The victim whimpered. The sob eased into a quiet moan.

I opened one eye and peeked. My mother, crumpled like a broken doll, cried softly on the floor near me. Her breathing sounded funny. Her cheeks glistened with blood and tears, and her broken nose destroyed the symmetry of her beautiful face. Radcliff-educated Melody Fitzpatrick, the daughter of an American diplomat, was a mass of crumpled flesh, blood, and bones. I closed my eyes at the sight. My mother had fallen in love with the monster who now assaulted her body and mind, blinded by the love that only comes once in a lifetime.

Of course, he wasn't a monster when my mother married him – that came later when he became a jihadi terrorist, filled with hate for all things Western, including his devoted wife.

I lay helpless for an eternity. I felt the sweat dry and evaporate from my body. When I opened my eyes, it was dawn. I was at home, in my townhome safe and sound in the outskirts of Washington DC. I was safe.

At least for now.

Chapter 1

I pulled my brand-new dark green Volvo Cross-County into my assigned spot at the Army War College in Bethesda, Maryland. I loved the vehicle and was proud to own it. I'd just retired from active duty in the United States Army after twenty years as an Army physician. After three months of full-time retirement, I'd figured out I had too much time on my hands. I didn't know how to cope with extra time, although my mother and her friends had kept me busy buying and furnishing a townhome close to Walter Reed Army hospital where I was a staff physician. I had also taken the time to hang out with Tessa, my Belgian Malinois, my retired war dog. Tessa had accompanied me on dozens of trips to the Middle East on official army business – even though most of the trips were business for her. Tessa had saved thousands of American lives by sniffing out IEDs and dirty bombs. Now, she traveled to work with me each day, made rounds with me as I visited my patients in the hospital, and laid on a rug next to my teaching lectern when I taught at the Army War College. In a sense, we were both happily retired.

I raced to my office and smiled at my personal administrative assistant. Frances was a tall woman, fiftyish, with iron-gray hair that she wore up in a bun every day. The defining word for Frances was "prim." She met the definition of straight-laced in every puritanical way. Her shoes were army issue and manly. Each day, she wore a white blouse with a round collar and a dark colored skirt. She pinned a circle pin on her collar every day. On cold days, she added a sweater to her austere outfit. On a special occasion, like a meeting with the brass and higher-ups, she added a colorful scarf to her attire and perhaps a pair of tiny earrings. Her earrings were almost always pearls, but on special occasions like my retirement party, she'd worn little blue stones. Frances' wardrobe offered few, if any, changes week after week. Nevertheless, she was a huge asset to me. She was efficient, dependable, and trust-worthy.

Her organizational skills extended far beyond those written in her job description - she kept me straight and made sure I attended all the meetings for the physician group faculty and war college professors. But, Frances' most incredible asset was her longevity in her job at the Army War College and her knowledge of the Agency's history and culture. She knew everyone – plus she knew everything about everyone – present, past, and future. She had an incredibly well-honed intuition that let her read people and their thoughts. Her insight was so uncanny, it sometimes made me nervous, and I had to beg her to stop.

Most of all, Frances was loyal, and her devotion to me was absolute. I loved her for that.

Frances stood, and gave me a curt smile as I walked into her office. "Good morning, Dr. Amon. May I get you some coffee?"

I flashed her a grin, "Frances, for the millionth time, please call me Sonia. If you don't, I'm gonna start calling you Franny Thomas. How'd you like that?"

Frances' eyes flashed disapproval. She didn't approve of casual banter. "I don't like that at all, Dr. Amon." Her voice was serious, her tone condemning, and her face displayed her displeasure.

I touched her shoulder. "I'm just teasing you, Frances. You know that."

Frances offered a half smile. "Yes, I suppose I do, Dr. Amon. I need to get used to your sense of humor. I've worked here for thirty-five years, and there has been little foolishness or humor associated with the Army War College or Walter Reed Hospital during my tenure."

I rolled my eyes and nodded. As much as I hated to admit it, she was correct. "Yes, I know. We'll need to change that in our little part of the world," I suggested. "Life is too hard not to have fun sometimes."

Frances took a deep breath and picked up her clipboard. "Well, you're wanted down in the main conference room on the third floor. It's the joint task force committee that overlooks the health of the Middle East, specifically Syria, as it relates to our troops and Syrian citizens. Here's your agenda."

As I took the two-page document from Frances, I noticed how closely clipped she kept her fingernails and how they mirrored her no-nonsense approach to life. I smiled when I saw she'd highlighted the agenda items that pertained to my mission and me. Public health was among them.

I continued to study the agenda as I left my office at the Army War College where I taught management and military science. It was not public knowledge, but the CIA owned part of me as well. My father was Syrian, and I was tall with dark eyes and long coppery- brown hair. I knew I could easily pass for an Arab woman because I had done it many times.

Before I retired from the United States Army three months ago, my specialty was working small, black ops missions, particularly in search of chemical and biological weapons. During my twenty years of service, I fought as a soldier, healed as a physician, and stole secrets as a covert spy.

I impatiently punched the elevator buttons repeatedly wishing the cumbersome car would appear. When the doors opened, I jumped in the elevator, grateful I was the only person on it. I pressed three and held my breath as the iron monster slowly descended four floors. I rushed down the blue-carpeted hallway and arrived at my meeting just in time.

Chapter 2

A tall Indian man stood, "Good afternoon, Dr. Amon. Welcome to our task force meeting. I'm Dr. Batak Basheer with the World Health Organization, and I'm in charge of this committee. I received notice a few weeks ago that you'd officially been assigned to all health matters - military and civilian - as they pertain to the Middle East region." The man smiled gently as he looked into my eyes.

I smiled. "Yes, yes, I knew that, and I'm honored to be on this task force. But, let me say, the entire Middle East is a large assignment."

Dr. Basheer smiled pleasantly. "Yeah, yes, it is. I understand you've spent time in the Middle East and more specifically, Syria." He raised his dark eyebrows and scrutinized me. With his bushy eyebrows, he reminded me of the Mad Hatter in *Alice in Wonderland*.

I smiled. "Yes, I was born in Syria. I've spent quite a bit of time on the ground there as well." I paused and flashed a smile as other physicians and military members entered, and sat down at the table, then I continued, "And also on the ground in many parts of the Middle East, both as an Army physician and as a child."

"You were born in Syria?" Dr. Basheer questioned as his eyebrows crawled even closer together.

"Yes, I was." I saw a few looks of confusion on my colleague's faces. The initial group had been joined by several others. "You see, my mother worked for the State Department and her father was assigned to the Embassy in Turkey. At any rate, she met my father; they fell in love and married. Later, they divorced, and I lived in various parts of the Middle East until I was eighteen years old." I'd given the committee the shorthand version. After all, I wasn't up for exposing the dirty family laundry on the first day.

"Oh my, what a wonderfully romantic story," exclaimed a dark-headed woman with the deepest shade of claret lipstick I'd ever seen. "I just love a romance!" She stood, came over, and offered me her hand. "I'm Dr. Carmen De-

Quentez, and I'm from the Center for Disease Control in Atlanta. I'm delighted to meet you."

I held my hand out to Carmen and immediately decided I liked her warmth, vitality, and the honest look in her eyes. She was quite beautiful. I knew that one day I'd have to tell her my parents' marriage was a love-tinged tragedy, and certainly not a love story. But today wasn't the day. In the meantime, I decided to keep quiet and study these people I'd be working with. "Thank you, Carmen," I said simply.

Dr. Basheer continued with introductions. "Dr. Amon, this is Dr. el Syed, the Iraqi health minister from Iraq and Dr. Agnosio, the health minister from Italy."

Dr. Agnosio was a short, stocky, distinguished-looking man with salt and pepper hair. I smiled a greeting, and he flirted with me with his dark eyes. Dr. el Syed and I exchanged platonic pleasantries.

"Lastly, Dr. Amon," Dr. Basheer said, "this is Mr. Jeff Hansen, who works with the State Department in the Middle East. He's a specialist on all things Middle Eastern."

I smiled at Jeff who winked at me. I'd known Jeff for years. He was the CIA handler who'd kept me alive and out of trouble as best he could for close to twenty years. I grinned at Jeff, and he gave me a secret smile and nodded.

"Pleased to meet you, Dr. Amon." Jeff greeted me with a coy smile. Jeff was handsome, over six feet tall with amazing hazel eyes, and was one of my dearest friends.

"Coffee?" Carmen asked as she headed toward the snack table against the far wall.

"That'd be great," I said. "Two sugars, please." One of the committee members looked down at Tessa. "Oh, by the way, this is Tessa. She's my retired war dog, and she has saved hundreds of lives – military and civilian. I've adopted her. We've made dozens of trips to the Middle East together, and she goes everywhere I go. We're inseparable." I leaned down and petted my beloved dog.

Dr. Basheer rubbed Tessa's ears. "Ah, a very fine partner indeed, Dr. Amon." He gave me a quizzical look. "Doesn't 'Sonia' mean 'wisdom' in Syrian culture?"

I nodded, pleased for some reason. I liked him. "Yes, Dr. Basheer, it does, and Amon means 'a good person.' It's hard to live up to the moniker of a 'wise, good person' but I do my best!" I smiled as my face reddened with embarrassment. My madly in love parents had named me before my father became radicalized and tried to kill my mother.

Carmen smiled, "Well, I already think you're a wise, good person, Sonia." She smiled at me. She had perfect, strong white teeth and beautiful long, shiny hair. "You've given me no reason to consider otherwise. Now, I suppose we should get to work."

Carmen led me to a chair next to hers and watched as Tessa moved into the corner of the room to take a nap. A moment later, Carmen introduced me to a late comer to the meeting. Dr. Betty Ballowe was a tall blonde and the WHO representative for Syria. She smiled at me as I watched Dr. Basheer walk toward the podium.

"My colleagues, as you know, many parts of the Middle East are in a full-scale health crisis. Today, we'll address Syria. War-torn Syria is a mess, and a health-care nightmare, just like other parts of the Middle East. Between the bombs and bullets, this poor country faces other growing threats, particularly disease outbreaks. Infections are rapidly mounting, and outbreaks are inevitable," Dr. Basheer's eyebrows arched in concern.

"Have there been any outbreaks?" Dr. Agnosio asked.

Dr. Basheer shook his head. "Fortunately, no, but there could be any day. The other concerns are, of course, the caches of biological and chemical weapons we're sure are there. Based on current knowledge and the duration of Syria's longstanding biological warfare program, we believe, both at the World Health Organization and at NATO, that some elements of the program may have advanced beyond the research and development stage. We think Syria may be capable of producing biological weapons."

The audience gasped!

Syria was able to produce chemical weapons. I shivered. I didn't know Syria had that capability. That scared me to death. I looked at Jeff, and he nodded slightly.

"You think Syria is prepared to release a biological weapon? I know they've released chemical weapons." Carmen's face and lipstick had both paled. "Since when?" She paused then asked, "And who would release them? The government? ISIS?"

Basheer shook his head. "We don't know. Maybe both. Nevertheless, we need to be prepared to meet a crisis such as this head on."

He turned and looked at me as though I was supposed to single-handedly stop a biological or chemical weapons attack. My anxiety escalated.

I raised my hand. "Dr. Basheer, I didn't know Syria had successfully weaponized any biological agents."

Dr. Basheer shook his head. "You are correct, Dr. Amon. It's not known if Syria has successfully weaponized biological agents for an effective delivery system, but Syria does possess conventional and chemical weapon systems that could be modified for biological agent use. We need to be cognizant of that, as part of the work of this task force is to anticipate catastrophic events and respond to them."

I nodded as panic seized me. I remembered my childhood home just fifteen minutes outside of Aleppo, in a beautiful area with shade trees, a swing set, toys, and pets. I'd had my very own playhouse on the second story of the barn where I had a day bed and all my toys. My mother and I used to play there together in my playroom every day. My nanna, my mother's helper, played with me too. The barn at my father's compound was special. If my father hadn't become a monster, my childhood would have been almost perfect. I wondered if my father had stockpiled chemical weapons back then and stored them in his barn.

"In addition to the concern for biological weapons, we must remember that all the risk factors that enhance the transmission of communicable diseases are present in Syria and throughout the Middle East as well," said Dr. Agnosio. "It's the perfect storm over there for a catastrophic outbreak event of epic proportion."

I saw a muscle in his jaw clench. He was handsome in many ways as were most Italian men. But his words were dire. I shivered again and rubbed the chill bumps off my arms. *Syria could be the root cause of a worldwide epidemic of any number of diseases that would escalate in the Middle East and spread to the rest of the world. Yes, that was entirely possible.*

My heart rate accelerated and my jaw clenched, but I managed to speak, "Yes, when we consider population movement both inside Syria and across borders, together with poor and deteriorating environmental health conditions, outbreaks are inevitable." I rubbed away more chill bumps. Everyone's eyes were on me. As the newbie on the committee, they were testing me.

"When were you last in Syria, Dr. Amon?" Dr. Basheer asked.

"I was there six months ago, shortly before my retirement from active duty and the public health systems had already collapsed." After a short pause, I added, "I think it's important that we remember the Middle East is not homogeneous. Countries are different, the terrain varies, governments are different, and religions are viewed differently. There are also so many different ethnicities that cross national boundaries and of course, there are tribal considerations that vary from country to country. We must be cognizant of that as we move toward rebuilding the health systems there. Things differ from the GCC countries through Iraq to Syria and Jordan."

"Good points, Dr. Amon. I read last week that vaccination rates have plummeted and almost half of the hospitals are closed. Many of the health care workers have gone to the front or have been killed by Assad's men," Dr. DeQuentez added.

"This is all true," Dr. el Syed added in a quiet voice. "Plus, there is a concern that a new SARS-related virus has a perfect breeding ground in Iraq and Syria."

Jeff Hansen spoke up. "Regions in parts of Syria are unstable, and leadership is unreliable. Your very worst nightmare could happen there at any time."

I nodded and added, "More than four million internally displaced Syrians are living in overcrowded and unsanitary conditions."

Dr. Betsy Ballowe intervened. "Dr. Amon is correct. Even at the less crowded refugee shelters, one toilet is being shared by fifty to seventy people." Her voice conveyed distress, and she paused a moment to sweep her long blonde hair behind her ears before she continued. "And the ratio of one toilet to seventy people is in a *good* area, such as Damascus." She paused to make her point. "In other areas of the country, it is much worse. Disease is spreading, and the death toll is rising. We must get in there quickly and do something!"

Dr. Basheer nodded; his face solemn as he made notes on his yellow legal pad. "What else do you know, Dr. Ballowe? I haven't been to Syria for several years."

I held my breath. I dreaded the answer. There were parts of my homeland where I hadn't been since I was a child.

"That's the gist of it, Dr. Basheer. The region is ripe for catastrophic outbreaks of diseases due to lack of vaccinations and unsanitary conditions." Dr. Ballowe made notes inside a gold-covered pad.

I stood and spoke, "What Dr. Ballowe has said has already happened. Syria has seen a resurgence of measles, mumps, chickenpox, and other childhood diseases that were formerly eradicated. Since the war, the vaccination programs have disbanded, and vaccination rates have plummeted. The fear of terrorism is high. Mothers and infants have been murdered on their way to get vaccinations," I said even though it sickened my stomach. "War against soldiers is one thing, but war against women, elders, and children is quite another." My pulse quickened as I thought about Muslim extremists murdering women and children on their way to the clinic to get a polio vaccine. I clenched my hands. I hated to feel helpless, and yet I'd felt helpless for a large part of my life.

From the podium, Dr. Basheer added, "Efforts to implement emergency vaccination campaigns have failed due to the terrorists. Syria was free of measles five years ago, but this year there have already been over five hundred cases." He sighed. "All in all, communicable disease is rising, especially in the refugee camps that are all over Syria and Iraq."

Dr. Agnosio tapped his pencil against the table, and a flush of anger reddened his face. "Given the scale of population movement both inside Syria and across borders, together with deteriorating environmental health conditions, outbreaks are inevitable."

I responded as calmly as I could. "We can only expect them to become worse. I find the new SARS-related virus that's emerged over Syria in the past year or so to be particularly troubling." I studied the faces around the table and realized I wasn't calming anybody. Tessa, asleep in the corner, was the only calm one.

Dr. Agnosio grimaced and stroked his short beard. "Yes, I agree. Syria has become a perfect breeding ground for epidemics of all kinds that will spread globally."

"What should we do?" I asked. "We must have a plan. What is the state of the public hospitals in the country?" It was clear that I had my work cut out for me.

Dr. Ballowe shook her head. "Not good. The World Health Organization estimates at least thirty-five percent of public hospitals are closed. In some areas, up to seventy percent of health workers have fled due to threats from the terrorists or to protect their own families. There is very little, if any, public or acute health care in the country for citizens."

"So, what we have are more than four million internally-displaced Syrians that are living in overcrowded and unsanitary conditions," Dr. Basheer added. "We must rebuild the public health system and send in medical people to organize immunization and basic medical-care clinics."

"I believe the United States military and our allies can help with that goal," Jeff suggested. "The State Department is concerned about public health in the Middle East, primarily Syria and Iraq, and is happy to offer assistance."

I smiled at Jeff. I knew he wanted me to go to Syria and help open medical clinics. We'd already spoken about it, and I was ready to leave any time.

Dr. Basheer nodded. "Thank you, Mr. Hansen. We've asked NATO to provide Humanitarian Aid and requested U.S. help to rebuild the health systems in Syria and Iraq. In the meantime, I'll look for opportunities to quickly assemble a few simple medical clinics that will offer immunizations and basic medical care."

I nodded. "Why don't I work with Dr. Ballowe, and we can decide which areas have the most need and where we should build the first few clinics. Perhaps Mr. Hansen can help us coordinate that with the military organizations currently peacekeeping in these two countries." I was breathless, but to establish a basic public health system in the country of my birth was a humbling opportunity for me. I needed to do it!

Jeff grinned at me and shook his head. I'd said exactly what he'd planned for me to do. I knew I was going to Syria in the next few months. Jeff and I worked well together. We'd gathered large amounts of covert information and Intel over the years. Some Intel I was sure we'd continue to collect, even in my retirement.

He gave me a thumbs up!

A shiver ran through me. I was always afraid in Syria because my father was Faisal Muhammed, widely considered a mass murderer by most of the free world. He was second in command of ISIS, the Islamic State of Iraq and Syria. He hated me because I'd escaped him. But then, sometimes I think he loved me too. There was no question that he was a conflicted man, but to me it was simple. He was a monster.

Chapter 3

The meeting was over when a young military aide tapped my shoulder. It was clear I had my work cut out for me. "Major Amon, you're needed in the emergency department. They've sent us a troop combatant from the Middle East. He's just arrived from Germany."

I nodded, a bit surprised. "All right, but can't any emergency physician attend to this man? What are his injuries?"

The aide shook his head. "I'm not sure. He was stabilized at Ramstein and then sent directly here. I think it may be someone you know. The soldier specifically asked for you." The young man's eyes drilled into mine. He wanted me to come with him.

I hid my trembling hands as I searched the face of the young man who handed me a written message. I glanced over the message. It was from the Emergency Clinic Manager, Avril Spencer. Avril was a good nurse and a great clinic manager. I read the message and nodded at the aide. "I'll be over there as soon as I can."

I quickly walked to my office and called Avril in the emergency department.

"Dr. Amon, you have a friend here, but I'm afraid he's very ill. He asked for you." Avril's voice was guarded.

I took a deep breath. I could imagine her soft, dark eyes carefully searching my face. For some reason, Avril had assigned herself as my protector. I wasn't sure why, but on some level, I appreciated it. Perhaps I needed all the protectors I could muster.

Fear crawled up my back. "Did you get a name?

"No, ma'am, I didn't. He's not doing well. I know he wants to talk to you as soon as he can." Avril paused. "He came from Syria, somewhere near Aleppo. He was in an explosion, and he's pretty beaten up."

The slivers of fear I felt a moment ago turned into a full-fledged, consuming rage. It permeated my body and flooded my senses. For a moment, I felt weak. I hated to feel weak or helpless.

"I'll be there as soon as I can." I wondered if he was one of Paul's men from his command post. I had a feeling he was, and my chest tightened. My fiancé, Colonel Paul Grayson, commanded a garrison outside of Aleppo.

"Take the elevator down. It's the quickest way to get over there," Avril directed. "See if you can hitch a ride with someone to save time."

"I will, thanks, Avril," I hung up the phone, picked up my briefcase, and waved goodbye to my faithful administrative assistant. I left my office at the Army War College where I teach military health care logistical management and military science. My specialty area was military health care and community health, but my "other" job was working small, covert CIA black ops missions. I'd been doing these missions for over ten years. My credentials as an Army physician got me anywhere in the world I needed to go, and my training in medicine and special ops enhanced my skills as an undercover operative. I also had a good grasp of the languages spoken in the Middle East because I'd grown up there. After all, my cruel, terrorist father, Faisal Muhammed, had kidnapped me from my American mother in the United States when I was almost five years old. I'd spent most of my childhood in Syria. My body went cold when I thought about my father. He was one of three major leaders in ISIS and pretty much the number one ISIS leader in Syria. He was responsible for much of the destruction of Aleppo and my hometown a few miles from the once majestic city. My heart cried when I remembered Aleppo. Gone was the beautiful ancient city, its splendor destroyed. The twelfth century castle had been demolished along with the Great Mosque and the bustling colorful souks of my childhood. The Aleppo I remember was gone. My heart ached at the memory of what was no more.

My father was a cruel, vicious man. He was spiteful and heartless. He'd never stopped searching for my mother or me and would thrust a knife in our chests as soon now, as he would have thirty years ago. I rubbed my arms up and down my body to rub away the fear and panic that consumed me whenever I heard his name.

I punched the elevator buttons impatiently and wished the cumbersome car would reach the bottom. It was only a short drive over to the Walter Reed emergency transport unit, but the parking was awful. Perhaps I could pick up a driver on the first floor. Yes, that's what I'd do. That would save me the time I'd waste looking for a parking space.

I jumped in the elevator grateful I was the only person on it. I punched the first floor and held my breath as the iron monster slowly descended four floors.

The hall traffic was busy when I exited the elevator. Between the Army War College and Walter Reed's medical center hospital staff and enlisted soldiers, it was hard to navigate to the support desk.

It was my lucky day. I saw a friend. One of my drivers. "Corporal Johns, I need a ride. Can you give me a ride over to the hospital? It's kind of an emergency." My voice was loud, and clear and I caught the young man's attention.

The handsome young soldier cupped his ear as though he couldn't hear me. He smiled. "Good morning, Major Amon." His blue eyes twinkled. "Where do you need to go?"

I smiled even though the inside of my stomach was on fire. "I need to get over to the hospital," I repeated. "There's a young man in the emergency transport department who has asked for me. He's not doing well," I admitted as my eyes searched the floor. I couldn't trust myself to keep my poise.

"Well then, Major, let's get moving," Corporal Jamie Johns said as we pushed our way into the busy corridor. He led me away from the traffic. "I've got a Jeep right up the road, about a block. We'll take the back way, so it shouldn't take us any time to get there, ma'am."

I sighed and was deeply grateful. I was lucky I'd run into Jamie. He was a good guy, and we'd served together in the Middle East. He'd been a medic until he'd been injured. Now, he was part of the motor pool.

Chapter 4

My patient was Captain Reid Handley. I knew him. He was one of Paul's men, and Paul was fond of the young soldier.

A sick feeling overcame me as I stared down at the thin, frail body of Captain Handley. I'd seen him six months ago during my last visit to Syria. The handsome young man had aged significantly. His skin was wrinkled and sallow, and his hair had turned gray. His weight was down by at least thirty pounds.

I smiled as our eyes locked, "Looks like you've lost some weight, old buddy. What's up? Is the food at the Aleppo Hilton no longer five-star?" I took his hand in mine and smiled into his tired face.

Reid smiled, but his voice was weak. "I'm certain the Aleppo Hilton never had five-star dining. But, all in all, the meal rations haven't changed at all and are just as tasty as ever." His smile was weak.

I picked up his medical record and glanced at the front sheet. "Well, the MREs could be worse, I guess. Looks like they brought you in through Ramstein. Remember any of that?"

Reid shook his head. "No, ma'am, not really." He paused, "I guess I was really beaten up."

"That I believe," I said with a smile. "But, we'll work hard to fix you up." I watched him carefully. I had a bad feeling about him. His eyes were blank. Shell-shocked perhaps? I didn't want to acknowledge the possibility of his diagnosis to myself.

Reid shook his head. "Nope, no, ma'am. Nothing at all," he repeated himself as he tightly closed his eyes. "The last thing I remember is giving the guys a hand signal to go left in an old building we were checkin' out." He closed his eyes as if a couple of sentences of conversation had worn him out. His hand brushed his forehead, and he kept his eyes closed for a moment.

I knew he was trying to black out the last few memories that lingered in his conscious mind. The memories just before his injury. I pulled the chair to the head of the bed, sat down, took his hand in mine, and asked, "Tell me what happened, Reid. Tell me what you can remember. Don't forget anything."

I saw anxiety cross his face. His pupils widened. He was frightened.

"We'll take it slow, and I'll be right here with you. I don't have anywhere I need to go." I touched his shoulder to offer as much reassurance as I could. I hated that I had to take Reid back through his nightmare.

Reid nodded and shrugged his shoulders. "It was just a normal day. A Friday. Colonel Grayson had asked us to search burned-out buildings about ten miles from the post. There was talk that insurgents were hiding there. We'd also heard ISIS worked out of the buildings. We'd gotten some Intel that a bunch of people had died there." Reid paused, short of breath. I waited until he was ready to continue and squeezed his hand.

"There were six of us plus Sam, our canine." He closed his eyes as if to visualize the incident better in his mind. I knew his mind wanted to explode and run as far away as it could. "We'd heard some chatter about the Emir's men being around from some of the locals." He paused to rest.

"Take your time, Reid. We've got lots of time," I encouraged him, but I could see him falter and tire before my eyes. I sat quietly and held his hand. I remembered back to the few days we'd shared together. Reid, Paul, and I were on leave in London about eighteen months ago. The three of us had had a wonderful time. We'd done a bunch of sight-seeing, ridden the London Eye, toured Buckingham Palace, visited the Tower of London, and had enjoyed way more Pimm's and soda than we should have. We'd also made our way to the naval yard and visited dozens of local pubs. I suppose it's pretty much what any GI does before he re-enters the war zone. Anyway, the three of us pledged to be friends forever. I'd served with them outside of Aleppo on my final deployment as active Army. Colonel Paul Grayson commanded the garrison outside of Aleppo. He was the love of my life, and we planned to marry soon. Reid was one of Paul's best officers in those days, and he was my friend. The three of us were inseparable.

Reid opened his eyes. "Seems like they, our Intel, were right and decided to kick it up a few notches. There were at least five or six bad guys there. They hid near the back." He sighed heavily and closed his eyes again.

I could see the signs of stress and illness in the Captain's body. Six months ago, Captain Reid Handley, a son of the great state of North Carolina and a graduate of North Carolina State University, had been one hundred and eighty-five pounds of steel muscle. What remained was a shadow of his former self. I flipped through his medical chart as he rested. A few minutes later, Reid fell asleep.

I continued to peruse his chart. I knew the Middle East. Syria, the land of my birth, was a hotbed of terror with both ISIS and Al Qaeda vying for leadership. These vicious terror groups, who united and worked together from time to time, were heinous, despicable lawless groups of criminals with no respect for human life. My mind wandered as I remembered the Aleppo of my childhood. And now, the ancient cultural city was gone.

I'd had three formal tours of duty there and had been in and out of Iran, Iraq, Turkey, and Syria dozens of times on special assignment. I knew just about every single shit hole over there. I knew the dangers and the evils that lurked in those burned out buildings. I recognized the uncertainty in every situation. I sensed the omnipresent evil. I understood as well as any soldier the price of life in that hellish part of the world. Life wasn't worth much. My heart ached for the men, women, and children of Syria.

Captain Handley opened his eyes. He smiled at me and gathered his thoughts. I watched as Reid moved around in his bed. I was stunned at how weak the former giant of a man was. I leaned over to help him onto his side when I saw the series of brown spots on his back and upper torso. I also noted he'd lost copious amounts of body hair. Fear formed around my heart. I knew why Reid looked as he did, why he was so ill. *Radiation. Reid had radiation poisoning. Those bastards had set off a dirty bomb with an RDD, a radiation distribution device.*

I sat quietly and let him proceed at his own pace, with some prompting on my part. "Then what happened, Reid? What can you remember?" My voice was soft as I carefully watched him.

The young officer shrugged his shoulders. "Then... then it happened. They got the drop on us. Somebody knew we were coming." He paused and collected his thoughts. "Sam, our dog, was in the room - ahead of us with his handler. He alerted, but it was too late." Reid covered his face with his hands. "The blast was huge. It blew me back out of the building."

"A dirty bomb?" I already knew the answer. *A dirty bomb with an RDD.*

He'd squeeze his eyes shut, but I saw the tears that oozed down his cheeks. "Yeah, a big one," he said in a hoarse whisper.

I nodded. "How many fatalities?"

Reid shook his head. "We lost Cooper and the other two. Another young kid, new to the squad died instantly. Another man... I don't know what happened to him." He shook his head. "Maybe he lived. I don't know."

I sighed as I scanned the papers in his file. "From what I have," I said as I read through the papers, "it seems you and the dog's handler were the only survivors."

A shadow moved across Reid's pale face. "What about the others, the locals? A lot of villagers were standin' around. Any idea if any of them lived? They were good people, I'd vouch for them." A look of sadness engulfed Reid's face.

I shook my head. "I don't know, but I imagine most of them did. I can check and let you know."

"Thank you, ma'am." Reid's voice was soft, almost inaudible.

I continued to read the chart. "Oh, it says here a few locals were knocked down by the noise, but there were few injuries from the blast," I assured him as I looked up from the folder. "Is there anything else you remember about the blast?"

Reid continued to stare at me. "Oh, it was a bad one. There were a lot of locals, good people, and the fear and panic on their faces was awful. There was a huge dust cloud and a lot of metal." He turned his head away from me. "I think the bomb was a 'dirty bomb.' I think it was a radiation dispersal device, an RDD."

I took a deep breath and continued, "Yeah. You're right. There's reason to believe the bomb was an RDD." Those bastards. I felt sick to my stomach as I assessed Reid. A quick look assured me that my guess of radiation poisoning was accurate. A dirty bomb can be a name for a radiological dispersal device. It sounds like this one had combined explosives, probably dynamite, with radioactive material. I touched Reid's shoulder. "How big was the dust cloud?"

His eyes locked with mine. "It was big, Sonia. It covered the entire nucleus of buildings, maybe forty or fifty feet in a square." He paused. "It was probably that wide, too, maybe wider. There's no question about the dirty part. We hustled the locals to run as fast as they could. We ran as well. People inside were encouraged to shelter in place. We begged the mothers to keep the kids inside, and asked them to cover their noses and mouths with a damp rag."

I nodded. "How close were you to the dust cloud?"

"I was right in the middle of it. I know I've got radiation poisoning. No question in my mind. They've already told me." He paused, "But I had to get out and help people. We went back in the building and pulled out a couple more guys. I don't know if they made it or not." Reid turned his head away from me. I gave him a couple of minutes to recover.

"When did you figure out you were hit?"

He shrugged his shoulders. "I don't know. Somebody told me and the next thing I knew, the medics had grabbed me. Then I think I lost consciousness."

"Do you have any open wounds, Reid?" My eyes assessed his body, alert for anything that was unusual. I looked for radiation burns.

The Captain pointed toward his left flank. "Yes, ma'am, back there at the top of my hip. It's a burn of some kind, and they're keeping it really greasy."

I grinned at him. "Mind if I take a look?"

"Not if you promise to keep a secret about all of my muscles being steel. Not many ladies know about it," his blue eyes twinkled at me which made painful hot tears behind my eyeballs. Even though he was most likely dying from terminal radiation poisoning, Captain Handley hadn't lost his sense of humor. I put my finger on my lips and said, "Mum's the word. I won't tell."

I gently turned him toward me to have a better look at his hip. Dismay flooded my mind. He had a large shrapnel wound, about seven inches in length that was deep. The skin around the edges of the wound was red in color due to the metal ions the shrapnel had introduced. The skin on his buttocks was reddened and warm. The odor stifled me. It was infected.

"What do you see back there, Doc. How does it look?" I could hear the pain in his voice.

"You have a hole in your tail, and that's exactly what it looks like." I kept my voice light. I didn't tell him I could see down to the bone.

Reid cleared his throat. "Yeah, I figured that. I think they pulled some shrapnel out in Germany. Or at least, I think I remember that."

"That'd be my guess." I pulled on some gloves and prodded around Reid's wound for a moment or so. I didn't feel anything hard or rocky that appeared to be more shrapnel. That was good. I was relieved. Hopefully, the wound would heal, but that would depend on the extent of his radiation exposure.

Just then, I felt a tap on my shoulder. I turned around and saw Major Cynthia DeWitt, a faculty member at the Armed Services University. She had six graduate students with her.

"Major Amon, do you mind if my students look at Captain Reid's wound? These are advanced practice nurses who're headed to the Middle East in a few months."

I smiled at Cynthia DeWitt. "Let me check with the Captain." I tapped Reid on the shoulder. His arm quivered with fatigue from holding his body up so I could inspect his flank. "Captain, do you mind if Major DeWitt and her graduate students look at your wound?"

"No, ma'am. That's okay," he said, but I could hear the fatigue in his voice.

I nodded to Cynthia and asked that they be quick. She asked if I'd do an introduction and an overview of Reid's situation.

"This is Captain Reid Handley, who recently returned from Syria via our friends at Ramstein in Germany. He and his men were looking through abandoned buildings when they encountered a dirty bomb. As best we can tell, the bomb was an RDD, a radiation deliverance device. Unfortunately, Captain Handley caught some shrapnel. Here, take a look." I urged the students to get closer.

"What does shrapnel do when it enters the skin?" A tall dark-headed nurse asked me as she studied Reid's wound.

"It hurts like hell," Reid joked. We all laughed.

"Potentially, a lot of damage," I replied. "Shrapnel is the general term for fragmentation of particles, metal shards, nails, glass, and ball bearings, anything hurtful that is thrown out of a bomb or shell when the object explodes. Shrapnel injuries are often dirty injuries and cause tremendous pain to patients." I paused. "They can embed deep into the flesh. You can see that here."

Several students nodded their heads. I continued, "The impact of a shrapnel injury depends on two factors - the speed of the fragments when they hit the body, and the area of the body the metal hits. As you can see, it can slice through flesh like a knife. It also has the ability to break and shatter bones."

"How's my injury look, Doc?" Captain Handley asked from the bed.

"Not too bad," I replied, my voice honest. "The wound has pretty clear edges, so we'll be able to get it healed up nicely. That said, it'll take a bit of time."

I waited a moment as the students rotated and inspected the Captain's injury.

"Captain," I said my voice light. "Would you like to turn over and look at these lovely young women who been gawking at your hind parts for the last ten minutes?"

"I suppose I might as well," Reid said with a short laugh as he rolled over. I saw him smile at the nurses.

"What'd you ladies think?" His eyes twinkled, and he winked at a lovely young woman with blonde hair. His southern accent was appealing.

"I think it looks good and I think it's gonna heal up just fine," the pretty, young blonde said as she clasped Reid's hand. "Thank you for letting us look."

"Thank you, Lieutenant Moyer," Reid said as he read her nametag. "It's not often I lay my butt out there on display, so consider yourself lucky." He smiled at her.

I felt the chemistry between the two young people and for some reason that made me feel good. Perhaps Lieutenant Moyer would come and visit Reid. That would make me feel good since I knew I'd probably have to leave DC for a trip to the Middle East soon.

Reid waved as the nurses filed past his bed. Lieutenant Moyer threw him a kiss. I had a feeling she'd be seeing him soon.

"So," I said as I looked down at him. "That was a nice surprise, wasn't it?"

Reid grinned. "Yup. That one nurse is pretty. I hope she visits me."

I nodded as I watched his eyes follow her. Then a shadow passed over his face. He leaned forward and motioned me down with his index finger. "Major, we gotta talk."

A feeling of dread pounded through me. I pushed my chair forward and lowered my head. "What, Reid? What is it?"

He motioned me closer with his index finger and whispered. "Colonel Grayson needs you, ma'am. He thinks they're cooking stuff up again. All of us do." Reid's voice was low, and his face was pale. "I think ISIS was cooking up stuff in the building we were looking in."

My heart fell to my toes. For a moment, I couldn't catch my breath. "Cooking stuff? Like before?" A couple of years ago, we'd destroyed a chemical weapons lab outside of Aleppo. My anxiety level skyrocketed and was so high I was dizzy. My mind whirled, and I held on to Reid's side rail for support. Then I remembered what they'd said at my meeting this morning.

He nodded slowly. "Yeah. Some kinda biological soup crap is our best guess."

I nodded. My heart thudded in my chest. "What makes you think so?"

"I saw it. The building we cleared, the one where I was injured. We had pics of before the explosion. There was lab equipment, microscopes, dishes, stuff like that everywhere. The bomb exploded just before we got into the main room. I suspect that was the lab." He paused. "I think they'd cooked up stuff and killed people with it, but I don't have proof."

I didn't respond as one nightmare after another swirled through my head.

Reid touched my knee. "Ma'am, you've gotta go. Paul needs you. Colonel Grayson needs your help. You know all that chemical stuff. You're an expert."

I smiled at him as a million horrific possibilities crashed through my mind. "I'm gonna go, Reid. Most likely tonight," I said in a gentle voice. "Will you promise to behave after I leave?"

Reid smiled broadly. "Thank goodness, ma'am. Now, I can rest easier." Reid laid back against his pillow, his face gray with exhaustion. "And, I'll behave as long as I have to stay in this bed. That's all I can promise." He winked at me and, for a moment, I saw the old Reid Handley. The good-looking dude in London.

"Well," I frowned, "I reckon that's just gonna have to do." I grinned at him. I was thankful Reid had his sense of humor. I remained with him for another few minutes before he fell into a deep slumber. He'd been a good soldier. The very best. I kissed him on his cheek before I left and ordered radiation levels. I figured his radiation level was two to three hundred RADs. His white blood cells were greatly decreased, and his chart from Ramstein chronicled radiation sickness. His prognosis was dependent on whether we could cure the infection which would be difficult because of the radiation.

I had Corporal Jamie Johns take me back to my office. I had a message from Jeff Hansen. "Wheels up at ten p.m."

I wondered what in the heck was going on, but I had a sick feeling that I knew.

Chapter 5

"Mom, mom, where are you?" It was about five in the afternoon when I walked in the front door of my mother's two-story townhouse. I made my way back to the kitchen, but she wasn't there. I checked my watch. It was five-fifteen. I speed-dialed her on my cell. I always worried about her. Especially since she was out of witness protection and my father could easily find her. I have a horde of friends that I put in charge of her every time I deploy. Tessa followed me and sniffed around in each room.

I was deeply relieved when she answered. "Mom, where are you? I came by to steal you for dinner. Are you available?"

"Hi, sweetie! Yes, I'm available, and I'm five minutes from home. Where should we go?" My mother sounded happy.

I loved the sound of my mother's voice. Her voice is soft, southern, and it completely wraps itself around you. I feel so fortunate to have her after so many years of not having her in my life. I never want that to go away, and yet I fear that may happen almost every day. I think my mother does as well.

"How about the Italian place up the road? I feel like Italian tonight. I've wanted a slice of their lasagna for two days," I admitted.

"Then Vito's it is!" I heard the smile in my mother's voice. "I'll be home in a couple of minutes."

I walked around my mother's beautifully decorated townhome. She had various collections of items she'd gathered from all over the world. Her exquisite taste was apparent. A few minutes later, her "new to her" but ten years old, Mercedes pulled into her garage. Seconds later, she was hugging me in the kitchen. Then she lavished hugs and cuddles on Tessa who grinned at her and happily licked her hand. Tessa loved my mother and my mother loved my dog. "What a lovely surprise, Sonia! I'm so excited you're here. Give me a few seconds to change clothes, and I'll be ready."

"Hang on a minute. There's no rush. I want to look at you," I smiled. "That's a beautiful blouse."

My mother's beautiful blue eyes smiled at me. She was dressed in a pale blue suit with a white silk blouse with just the right amount of lace for a day job. Melody was a linguistics expert at the State Department in downtown Washington DC. She was good at her job. She was currently researching "lying" and examining voice tapes for inflections and changes in speech when people lied.

"Thank you, Sonia. I went shopping a few days ago. Caught a great sale and got a few other things too."

I nodded. My mother was tiny, petite with pale, long blonde hair that she wore in a French Twist every day she went to work. When she was at home, she often wore it loose. Her hair was long and wavy. It was hard to believe she was almost sixty years old. But, the Fitzpatrick's lived long lives. Her parents, my grandparents, still lived in Georgetown and my grandfather still worked. Melody's face was unlined, and she had the energy of someone half her age, a fact she contributed to hours spent in the gym and swimming. In truth, my mother had lived parts of her life in hell. We'd been separated most of my childhood. For her own protection, she'd been hidden from my father in the Witness Protection program for thirteen years. She'd come out from witness protection when I'd returned to the United States at the age of eighteen.

"Well, with your permission, I'm gonna go upstairs, change into jeans and then we can go out."

"Okay. Good plan," I agreed as I took a seat in the living room. Tessa stayed on the cool tile floor in the kitchen.

My mind wandered. I can remember when I was about twelve years old and living in my father's house outside of Aleppo. I cried because I couldn't remember what my mother looked like. I couldn't remember that, but I always remembered her smell. She'd always smelled of violets, and she still did. Her perfume had been inscribed into my mind ever since I was born, and in all the years I'd been away from her, I'd never forgotten the scent.

My mother came downstairs and caught me daydreaming. "Honey, you look great!" There's no question that my mother is my greatest admirer. Even though I'm rarely presentable, I don't think she's ever told me I looked less than perfect. "I love those jeans!"

I hugged her. "Yeah, I love 'em too! I ordered them from Amazon, and I'm delighted they're long enough. I got them the other day and," I winked at her and kissed her cheek, "I picked up a pair for you, too!" I laughed. "Yeah, they came in baby-size!"

She giggled. "Baby-size? I'm a little bigger than that," she admonished as she pulled her long hair on top of her head in a loose chignon. Her blue eyes shined with happiness.

"Well, maybe not 'baby-size,' but most definitely petite."

My mother shook her head. "Really, Sonia, you make it sound like you're an Amazon woman. You're not too tall. You're a perfect size," she assured me. "In my next life, I want to come back tall," my mother said. "Just so I can reach stuff on the third shelf."

I laughed at her. I knew we could never get the thirteen years that my horrific father held me captive in Syria back, but ever since I'd escaped from him at the age of eighteen, we'd worked hard at recapturing all we could. "You're right. I've just always wanted to be petite like you," I said as I caught a look at my five-foot ten-inch self in her hall mirror. We were visual opposites, I was tall with dark hair and deep brown eyes, and my mother was a perfect, petite English rose. It's easy to see why my Syrian father fell in love with her. She was exotic, different from what he was used to in his country.

A half an hour later, I sat across the table from my mother as we shared a bottle of red wine at Vito's Italian Restaurant. I'd chosen a French Malbec.

My mother picked up the bottle, "This wine is really good, Sonia. Have you had this vintage before?"

I set my wine glass down on the snow-white tablecloth. "No, I haven't, but I like Malbec now. I've been buying it for a couple of months." I picked up my glass and held it toward the light. "This one has a beautiful red color and a great nose."

My mother smiled and we clicked glasses. "Everything about this wine and this evening is lovely. I'm so glad you retired from active duty and will be around more!" My mother was happy, and her eyes glistened in the low light.

My spirits plummeted. *Here it comes. I've gotta tell her now.* "Yep, that's true for the most part... but," I locked eyes with her, "I'm still going to have to travel. In fact, I'm leaving tonight. I have to go back to the Middle East to check out a few things, tie up some loose ends, and plan a way to quickly build some medical clinics."

My mother's face crumbled, and she sat her glass of wine on the table. "You're leaving tonight? Why so sudden? Is something wrong?" I saw fear flicker across her face. In my mother's mind, everything about the Middle East was cruel, harsh, and uncivilized. Her time there, living and being subjected to my father's anger and his people, most of whom had mistreated her at his order, terrified her. Her face was white with fear, and her eyes were panicked.

I reached for her hand. "Mom, it's just a quick trip in to examine Syria's public health system, particularly around Aleppo and in that region. I'm on a task force sponsored by the World Health Organization to improve the health in the Middle East."

My mother shook her head. "Can't someone else do it? Certainly, someone else has experience there. Another doctor?" My mother's eyes were filled with angst. It was a nightmare for her each time I went there. It was a nightmare for me as well, but I never admitted that to anyone.

"Nope, just me," I tried to calm her as I reached for her hand. "I shouldn't be gone more than a couple of weeks." I watched as she processed this information.

She shook her head and asked again. "But why you? Why can't another physician go over there and do the same thing? Even more than that, why send a doctor at all. A business person could set up a clinic." My mother's hands were clasped so tightly that her fingernails were blanched white.

I shrugged my shoulders. "It's me because I have more experience in Iraq and Syria than most army physicians. And we need a physician because we're gonna set up a few medical clinics before a bunch of diseases break out." My voice was matter-of-fact.

My mother nodded but didn't respond. She chewed her food slowly.

I knew she was worried because she was afraid Faisal would "get" me, but seriously, I'd been protected over there for years.

"Don't forget that I was in charge of the medical facilities there for the last three years," I reminded her gently. "And don't worry, Faisal isn't gonna get me. With a little luck, he's forgotten that I even exist," I grinned, knowing there was no way my monster father would ever forget me. I represented a failure to him, and he had vowed before the world never to fail at anything. He had this love/hate relationship with me. Every now and then, he'd send me flowers for no reason. I always knew they were from him because Jeff traced the order on the internet for me. I never acknowledged them.

My mother's blue eyes flashed in anger. "He'll always try to capture you and bring you back into his world," she glared at me. "And, so far, it's only been through the grace of God that your father, Mr. ISIS, or whoever he is now, hasn't had his goons take you and cut you into little bits and return you via the U.S. mail." Her hands fluttered over the table.

I grabbed her hands to calm her. I didn't say anything, possibly for several reasons. Faisal Muhammed would have captured me and sent me home in pieces if he'd been so inclined. I suppose I was off his radar for some reason at this moment. I knew there was a standing reward on my head for anyone with any information about me whenever I returned to the Middle East. He'd pay millions of dollars for me. The Army was aware of that, and my mother knew as well, so there was no way to escape that reality. I just had to keep it in check, so it didn't eat away at my mother or me.

"Well, he hasn't gotten me yet, and I haven't heard much about him lately." I picked up the wine bottle and busied myself to slow my furiously beating heart. I never wanted to show fear of my father in front of Melody. I knew it frightened her.

I saw my mother reach down for her pocketbook. I watched her remove a Kleenex from a plastic container. I shook my head and smiled to myself. She was such a lady. Where had I come from? I was semi-barbarian – unless, of course, it was a sterile wound or something medical. I'd as soon use a paper towel as a Kleenex to blow my nose. I guess it was because I was raised by Barbarians in Syria for most of my childhood.

My mother and I had escaped my father shortly after my third birthday. I had watched as Faisal had beaten my mother senseless a few nights before. It's the dream that I have almost every night until I wake up soaking wet with sweat and fear. It's the memory that shattered my life.

We'd had the help of an old man, a village elder, who'd lived in the countryside near my father's home. He'd loaded us in his truck and driven many miles to meet some American soldiers. I'm sure my diplomat grandfather, Randolph Fitzgerald, had arranged for our escape. The Americans had transferred us into another truck and taken us to an airfield where we'd been placed on a plane to the United States.

I was three years old when we returned to the United States. My mother was twenty-eight years old. The government had kept us in protective security for about eighteen months, until chatter had died down about how angry Faisal was about losing his wife and child. My grandfather had spent most of his fortune keeping us safe. Even now, his estate kept my mother safe.

Unfortunately, my father has a lot of connections and a very long arm. Six months after we'd left protective custody and moved to our first home, I was taken from my elementary school during recess. I remember it well. The school secretary had come out to find me. She had a note in her hand, and there was a tall, dark gentleman with her. "Sonia, your mother asked that this gentleman bring you home. I think you have unexpected company," she'd said with a smile.

I shook my head in protest, but by this time, the tall Muslim had my small hand in his steel clasp. He turned, and we walked across the street to a black limo that waited for us. A few hours later, we went through customs at Dulles airport. The next day, I was back in Syria with my father who at this point could hardly stand me because of my American ways. I lived with my father in his compound until I was eighteen years old when I finally escaped back to America with the help of a village shaman. I joined the United States Army because I was afraid of my terrorist father, who was a major leader of the Islamic State, an ISIS Emir. I believed that the Army could keep me safe and so far, they had.

I stared into my mother's deep blue eyes, now veiled with pain and fear. "Mom, I promise you. I'll be safe. Only a handful of people know where I'm going. Part of my job at Walter Reed is advising the World Health Organization and NATO on the health conditions of countries that I'm familiar with, and the Middle East countries and Syria, are certainly among of them. I have a responsibility to the CDC, the WHO, and the United States military."

My mother's blue eyes were filled with tears. "Do you think he knows you'll be there?"

I shook my head. "I would hardly think so. The last thing Faisal is interested in is healthcare for the citizens in Syria, especially since he and his buddy, Assad, devastated the former health care system."

My mother smiled through her tears. She looked relieved. "I suppose you're right. I guess I'm just selfish - I want you for myself."

I grinned. "Oh, is that right? Well, I'll be back in a few weeks, and we can do whatever you'd like. I promise." I looked up as our waitress appeared with my lasagna and my mother's Fettuccine Alfredo. "Yum, that smells wonderful."

I waited for the waitress to serve us. "Wow, this is gonna be delicious."

My dinner was excellent, the salad crisp and fresh, and the bread freshly baked. I don't know how they made the sauce at this restaurant, but it's the best red sauce I've ever had.

After a few bites of her fettuccine, my mother spoke. "How long do you think you'll be gone?"

I shook my head. "I don't know for sure, but I would imagine about two to three weeks."

"That long?" My mother looked surprised.

I nodded. "I've got to travel to most of the areas to determine the needs they have. The conditions there are horrific. So many women and children are in refugee camps, and there's no safe or sanitary drinking water, much less healthcare. I'll need to vaccinate as many people as I possibly can."

"Will other physicians be with you?" I knew my mother hated for me to be in the country with the monster she considered my father to be. To be honest, I'd seen things he was responsible for, and he was worse than a monster.

I nodded. "I don't know about other physicians, but I'll have trained Army medics which is probably better. I plan to set up some temporary healthcare clinics and take lots of vaccines with us. What we're trying to do is prevent a global epidemic of smallpox, polio, or other communicable diseases." *And, stop the bad guys from cooking up a chemical soup designed to kill all of us.* That part I didn't mention. My mother would have a stroke if she realized what I truly did for a living and had done throughout my years with the American military.

"Will you be with Jeff?" My mother liked Jeff Hansen. Sometimes the three of us had dinner together. She knew Jeff Hansen always watched out for me, and she trusted him to have my back.

I grinned and nodded. "Yeah, I'll fly over with Jeff, and he'll be my contact. He'll likely travel with me most of the time." I stopped and smiled at the waiter who refilled our water glasses. "But, best of all, I'll get to see Paul. I'll be housed at Paul's military command outside of Aleppo."

My mother's smile widened. "Ah, Paul. You'll be with the man you love." She winked at me. "Now, I can see why you don't mind the trip. Between Paul and Jeff, I think you'll be fine." Her face relaxed.

I blushed. My mother knew I loved Colonel Paul Grayson.

"Will you give Paul a hug for me and tell him I'm putting him in charge of you?" Melody grinned at me.

I nodded. "I absolutely will. He'll be delighted to hear that." I laughed, and so did my mother.

"Well, you know where I am when you get back. Will you try to call me from over there?" Suddenly, my energetic mother looked tired as reality set in.

"I absolutely will. No question. I'll have several phones, so if you get one with a number you don't recognize, that could be me as well."

My mother nodded. "Should we have dessert? Do you have time?"

"I absolutely do. And I want the double fudge brownie cake."

My mother shook her head. "You're incorrigible and a chocoholic!"

I gave her my dumb smile. "Yep, you got that one right."

Chapter 6

Colonel Paul Grayson walked out of the Officer's Mess tent at the American military post he commanded just to the south of the war-torn city of Aleppo. Dinner had been pretty good, especially for food in the Middle East. He waved at a couple of his junior officers enjoying a drink on the "veranda," a wooden deck off the Officer's Mess, the men likened to the genteel living of the deep South.

Paul Grayson was a Southerner, born and raised in South Carolina. He'd graduated from the Citadel and entered the United States Army at the age of twenty-two with a college degree. He had turned down his first opportunity for military retirement, mainly because he wasn't sure what he would do with his time. However, since then, he'd met and fallen in love with the beautiful Sonia Amon, a former Army Major, physician, and daughter of jihadist Emir Faisal Muhammed. Colonel Grayson knew he wanted to marry the beautiful doctor within minutes of meeting her. Now, he planned to retire at the end of his current tour in the Middle East that ended in four months. The two planned to marry and live in Northern Virginia.

"Evening, men. What's going on?" he asked as he took a seat at the table on the veranda and placed his can of beer on the table.

"Evening, Colonel. How was dinner?" One of his men asked as he moved his chair over to make room for his commanding officer.

Paul cracked a smile. "It was as good as it ever is, consistent if nothing else. Anything going on around here?"

Sergeant Snead shot a glance over at his Lieutenant and nodded.

Colonel Grayson caught the look and turned his attention to Lieutenant Jenkins. "What's up, Jenkins? Do we have trouble on the horizon?"

Jenkins took a swig of his beer. "Yeah. I'm afraid we might. Eight of us took two trucks and went on patrol today. We backtracked from where we were the other day when we caught the dirty bomb. We picked through the rubble again." He scratched the side of his face and swatted an insect. His face was red and sweaty.

Colonel Grayson leaned in toward the center of the table. "Yeah, what'd you find?" Grayson's face was lined. For a moment, he looked much older than his forty-five years.

Jenkins shook his head. "More of the same, Colonel. We picked up a lot of lab equipment. Some of the tubes have residue in them, so I think we should send them for testing. There were a bunch of glass bottles that didn't blow up in the explosion." He shook his head. "That's about it."

Grayson locked eyes with Jenkins. "Doesn't sound good to me."

Jenkins shook his head. "Nah. I agree. When I see that kinda stuff, it makes me think for sure the Islamic State is cooking up chemical or biological weapons. There were all kinds of broken glass bottles with the universal poison symbol on them." He stamped his cigarette out on the wood deck, picked up the butt, and put it in his pocket.

Grayson nodded. "Yeah, what else? Did you find anything else?"

Jenkins turned to a corporal sitting diagonally across from him. "Tell him what else we found, Corporal Scully. Bad as it is, he has to know."

Scully locked eyes with the colonel "Sir, we found a large open grave filled with dead Syrians. Most of the victims were the elderly, women, and children. I think whatever the extremists made was tested on these civilians."

Colonel Grayson's heart raced. He clenched his fist. He had to call in reinforcements. "An open grave? Why would they leave the grave open?" Fear settled in his gut.

Scully shook his head. "Don't know, Sir. It's a mystery to me. They'd thrown a few canvas tarps over the bodies. The grave was shallow." He hesitated. "It was a bad sight, Sir. Hard to look at."

Grayson shook his head. The terrorists were barbaric. "How many dead civilians?"

"I'd say about seventy or so; wouldn't you, Lieutenant?" Scully asked as he looked over at Jenkins.

"Yeah, I'd say so. At least that many. They killed a lot of kids. They're a sick bunch of bastards, no question."

The other men around the table nodded in agreement.

Corporal Scully continued, "We covered the bodies and buried them as best we could, Colonel." He picked up his beer and took another long drink, but Lieutenant Jenkins knew that all the beer in the world would never wipe out the atrocities young Corporal Scully had seen in the last four months.

"How long do you think they've been dead?" Grayson studied the nails in the wooden deck. His face was closed, but Scully could see a muscle twitch in his jaw.

Jenkins shrugged his shoulders. "Hard to say in this heat. Maybe five days to a week. It was a mess. I'd say they were killed just before the dirty bomb went off the other day."

"Did you turn in the paperwork on this? I need to review it and contact headquarters." Grayson's mouth twisted.

Scully nodded and looked over at Lieutenant Jenkins. "Should be ready most anytime, Sir. Want me to bring it to you directly?"

"Yeah. I'll be in my office," Grayson said as he drained his beer, crushed the can, and threw it in the trash. "You see anybody else out there? We need to get a few more patrols together and search more. They've probably moved this lab, but I think they're close and are planning something chemical or biological. "At least, that's my best guess."

Scully paled a bit under his tan. "I hope not, sir."

"Well, I'd sure like to know what killed all of those people." Captain Grayson shook his head.

"Nope. We didn't see nobody, but I can guarantee you there were dozens of eyes on us. They had a bead on us as soon as we reached the bombsite and watched us the entire time we were there." Jenkins looked at the men around the table. "Right, men? You felt those eyes on your backs."

"Sure did, Sir," an enlisted man reported. Grayson watched the other men nod. The enlisted man was so angry that he kicked the deck.

"Yeah. Bring the paperwork to headquarters," Jenkins directed Scully.

Grayson nodded at his men. "Carry on. I've work to do."

His men saluted him as he walked off toward headquarters.

This wasn't feeling at all good. Colonel Grayson had ominous feelings about all of this - the dirty bomb, the makeshift weapons lab, the dead Syrians - he needed more help - perhaps as many as three additional platoons. They were a prime target for attack. Sitting ducks, some would say.

Chapter 7

I sat across from Jeff Hansen, my CIA handler, drinking coffee at Langley. Jeff had been my handler for almost my entire Army career. He was one of the few people who knew my real identity. Jeff knew who my father was. Jeff knew how evil and hideous Faisal Muhammed was. My father had promised to kill me years ago. There'd been some near misses, and Jeff knew he'd never give up. Jeff always kept an ear out to hear what Faisal was up to. He'd been assigned to the Middle East desk his entire CIA career.

I warmed my hands with my cup. "So, what do you think is going on over there?"

Jeff grinned and his nose wrinkled. "Same old, same old. Faisal's acting up; we heard he's working on a chemical or biological attack. Nothing specific."

I rubbed chill bumps off my arms. "Yeah. That's what we heard this morning. What do you think?"

Jeff was contemplative. "I think we simply don't know. We've known for years that there's a cache of chemical weapons in Syria. I'd guess that he's gonna move with what he has."

I nodded, and my stomach burned from the coffee. "I can confirm that Lieutenant Reid Handley has radiation poisoning he acquired when terrorists tossed a dirty bomb a few days ago. He also told me he thinks the Islamic State is cooking up some chemical weapons, 'chemical soup,' as he calls it. Have you heard anything?"

Jeff nodded his head. "Yeah. The Lieutenant is correct. The unfriendlies find it increasingly easy to launch attacks using biological weapons now. Extremists have greater access than ever to the information and technology needed to create and spread germ warfare and other biological weapons. And, what they don't have, they steal."

My body chilled with fear. "What's so much easier now than before?"

Jeff shook his head and spread his hands, palms upward. "The Islamic State has recruited or captured several prominent scientists who made their job much easier. Other factors that make the use of these weapons easier include the availability of the formulas and other information that's easily available on the Internet." His face was grim. "The kid down the street could make chemical weapons now."

My eyes dilated, and I had a chill. I nodded. "Of course, they can. There are several dozen recipes on the Internet on how to make crack cocaine." I pause for a moment. "What do you think about the RDD, the radiation dispersal with the dirty bomb? Were you aware that ISIS was using these radiological dispersal devices?"

Jeff nodded. "Yeah. We've seen more of that. Both in Syria and in Iraq. We're seeing more radiation where ISIS is, so it's logical there are more radiation dispersal bombs in Syria." As an afterthought, Jeff added, "They've actually been using radioactive materials since the early days of Al Qaeda."

I winced. "This is a dreadful war. I don't know if it'll ever stop. As soon as we get ahead of them, something else happens, and they gain more power and momentum than we do."

Jeff eased back into his chair. "Yeah, it does seem that way. These terror groups are well financed. A new report out of the United Kingdom suggests terrorist organizations make millions of dollars every day, an easy hundred million a year on oil sales, not to mention the twenty or thirty million or so they make every year on kidnappings."

"Terrific," I scowled. I was tired, and I blamed my overloaded carbohydrate dinner on the fatigue. I hadn't even left Washington DC, and I was pooped. I yawned and put my hair up with a clip. "Is there any new information from the search last week near Aleppo that injured Lieutenant Handley?"

My handler shoved a piece of paper across the table toward me. "Yeah. This came in about half an hour ago. Colonel Grayson sent another unit back there today to search for more evidence of a potential chemical or biological attack. They found a mass grave of about seventy or so Syrian civilians who had been forced to sample the brew, so to speak. We buried them." I heard Jeff curse under his breath.

My dinner moved up my esophagus, and for a moment, I thought I'd be ill. I back swallowed. I wondered if this could get any worse, but then chided myself because I knew it could. Anger shot through my body and lit up my limbic system. "What kind of 'brew?' Did they poison or gas them?" I was so furious that I could hardly speak. I was, in effect, half-Syrian even though I was an American citizen. It was the country of my birth, and although I felt no allegiance to their government, I did have an allegiance to the Syrian people. It hurt me to see my country killing their own people. It was barbaric. It was terror. It was wrong.

Jeff watched me carefully. He'd been my handler for a long time. In some respects, we'd sort of grown up together. Jeff had been an army officer but had permanently moved over to the CIA as conditions in the Middle East worsened after September 11. Jeff eventually left the Army and moved over to the Agency where he'd been ever since. As I said, he knew Faisal Muhammed was my father. Of course, all my commanding officers throughout my military career had known. After all, having me as a soldier put their units in more danger. It was no secret that my father would pay a million dollars to anyone who had information about me. He'd probably pay a billion to whoever brought me to him alive.

"It's unclear how they died, and we're not sure what they used. It could have been something they had the people ingest, like a pill or something, but it could also have been a poisonous gas." He paused for a moment, touched my shoulder, and continued, "Listen to me, Sonia. We've had this conversation before. These are not your people. Your father may be Syrian, and he may be one of the worst, most-wanted men alive, but in truth, he really isn't your father, and these killers are not your countrymen."

I nodded, but still felt the need to protect innocent civilians. "Who is responsible for all of this? Have the bed partners changed much since I retired six months ago? That's one of the problems with the Middle East. No one ever knows who supports who and which men are members of which terrorist group."

Jeff grinned and shrugged his shoulders. "We'll never know for sure who supports who. I think that changes almost daily."

I nodded. I was so angry I could feel a vein throbbing in my neck. "So, do we think ISIS or President al-Assad killed these people? We know al-Assad poisons people. Remember Damascus." I stopped and fidgeted in my chair. My face flashed anger. It was bad enough to know people wanted to poison and kill you, but for some reason, at least for me, I needed to know who wanted to do it.

Jeff spread his hands wide and shook his head - a signal to me that he didn't know. And trust me, if this guy didn't know, I'm sure no one did. I sat there in sheer misery as I waited for him to formulate his response to me. I shook my head.

He wiped the sweat off his forehead with his handkerchief. It wasn't even hot. I'd been cool ever since I'd been in the airplane hangar. As a matter of fact, I'd even had a few chill bumps which I rubbed away from my forearms.

"I honestly don't know, Sonia, but my guess is that it's the Islamic State. ISIS seems to be the big guys these days with the most money and fighters. You know how barbaric their methods are. Several terror groups have succumbed to them. The Islamic State is a caliphate, and that offers it some legitimacy."

I shook my head. I was a Muslim. A peaceful Muslim, but still a Muslim. "A caliphate is an Islamic State under the leadership of the person considered as a religious successor to the Islamic prophet Muhammad. This is a leader of the entire community." I glared at him. I'm sure my dark eyes glittered with anger.

Jeff gave me a close-lipped smile and raised his eyebrow. "Now, who does that make you think of?" He had a gleam in his blue eyes.

"I shook my head. "Not my father! No way, Faisal..." I stopped for a moment. "Actually, there's a radical Sunni Islamic group that's seized large amounts of territory in eastern Syria and northern and western Iraq."

Jeff nodded. "That's true. And they're growing in strength and numbers, no matter what the White House thinks, they're still a formidable enemy."

I nodded. "What about ISIS?"

"ISIS, or the Islamic State of Iraq and Syria, formed out of Al Qaeda after they invaded Syria in 2013. So," he paused, "ISIS has pretty much absorbed Al Qaeda in Syria."

I nodded wearily. I pretty much knew the story. It didn't sound like much had changed. "Tell me again how the Islamic State originated."

Jeff settled back in his chair and surveyed the grounds in his coffee cup. The Islamic State traces its roots back to the terrorists who pledged allegiance to Osama bin Laden and formed Al Qaeda in Iraq – a major force of the insurgency. After Abu Zawarid's death, Al Qaeda created an umbrella organization, known as the Islamic State. Fortunately, it was weakened by U.S. forces. At any rate, the U.S. has continued to push ISIS back until it no longer operates in much of the populated areas of Iraq and Syria. That said, the Islamic State has captured new territories in Syria and Iraq."

I nodded. I remembered this now. "How many people live under full or partial control of ISIS?" I asked as I stood and walked around the room to stretch my legs.

Jeff shrugged his shoulders. "I don't know. Nobody knows. Everyone has an estimate, and we figure around ten or twelve million. We believe they have anywhere between twenty to thirty thousand fighters in Iraq and Syria, but it could be much more. It's also important to note they have many fighters that are foreign fighters, many from the United States." Jeff gave me a sideways glance.

I shook my head. There was no question that the Islamic State was powerful and even with all the United States firepower, they continued to prosper. "This war is never going to end. The United States will be fighting this war when you and I are long dead, Jeff."

He nodded. "Remember, ISIS is a caliphate based on Sharia Law and is attractive to lots of ideologues and dreamers. And, you're right. It seems like a forever war. It's not often that an enemy is as well-financed as these guys."

I yawned and checked my cell phone. "It's after midnight. Shouldn't we be leaving soon? I was hoping for a good night's sleep on the way over."

Jeff held up his finger. "Hang on; let me check with the pilot. It shouldn't be too much longer."

I put my hands behind my head and leaned back in my metal chair. I'd be happy to get there. I hadn't seen Paul for over four months. Nevertheless, I hated it that I had to return to the unfriendly mountainous terrain that was so full of war with so little hope.

I must've fallen asleep for a few moments. Jeff shook my shoulder. "Heads up, Sonia. Wheels are up in ten minutes. We have a long trip." Jeff grinned and winked. "Let's go."

My eyes registered surprise. "What? You're going? You've never deployed with me before. Who's gonna be my handler stateside?"

Jeff roared with laughter. "Me. That's who. I've been in Afghanistan, Iraq and Syria at the same time you've been there. You've just never seen me."

I cocked my head. "Yeah. Then why don't I see you?" Of course, I knew why, but I was playing with him. Jeff and I went back a long way.

Jeff laughed. I loved it when he laughed. He had a rich, delicious baritone laugh. I suppose the fact that he didn't laugh often made it more special. He was also good-looking in a boyish sort of way.

He grinned at me and answered. "Generally, because I'm working hard to keep you alive, Sonia. That's what I do. Gather intelligence and keep your butt breathing."

"And, I truly appreciate that, Jeff!" I laughed. "But, is something different this time? I've had a funny feeling."

"What do you mean by a feeling? Like a sixth sense?" Jeff's dark eyes pierced mine and held them for a second. Jeff was an old warrior, and old warriors believed in funny feelings and intuition. We both knew the Army believed in the concept of sixth sense and had developed a program that detailed a "sixth sense" or a "Spidey sense."

I gave Jeff a steady look. "Tell me about the sixth sense again. I need a refresher." I said as I settled into my seat.

Jeff took a breath and began. "According to the Pentagon, the 'sixth sense' program was born of analyzed field reports from the war experience that included a 2006 incident in Iraq when a staff sergeant used intuition and prevented carnage from an IED."

"Oh, now I remember. The sergeant anticipated or 'felt' the improvised explosive device incident. It's coming back to me now."

Jeff nodded. "Yeah. The Pentagon reported that oftentimes these reports from the field detailed a 'sixth sense' or 'Spidey sense' that alerted them to an impending attack or IED, or bomb, or some catastrophic event. The sense allowed them to respond to a novel situation without consciously analyzing the situation."

I shook my head. "No. I can't call it a sixth sense thing. I feel something's different – that something different is gonna happen."

Jeff held my stare. His heart raced. I'd never said this prior to a deployment. "What's gonna be different? Can you feel something specific?"

I shook my head. "Nah, not really. Just that something's gonna be different. Has something happened over there I don't know about?"

He shook his head. "Nope. No. Not yet. But I think the entire geographic area around Aleppo is gonna blow open soon."

My heart almost stopped. I broke out in a cold sweat. "Blow open? What do you mean? I don't understand." I tried to keep any sound of hysteria out of my voice, but my insides were on fire. "Blow open how?" *My God, Paul's command is in that area, and I have a bunch of friends in that area.*

Jeff shrugged his shoulders. "Not sure yet, but something's gonna happen." I heard a tone of frustration in his voice.

"Terrific," I said, my voice sarcastic as I picked up my duffel bag. "Let's get out of here. Let's hit it."

Jeff picked up his pack. "Let those thoughts percolate, Sonia. It could be the difference between life and death."

I nodded and pressed through the door. Screw this trip, screw the Army, but most of all screw my horrific terrorist father. Whatever was up would have his long touch of evil damnation.

It's gonna be a long night.

Chapter 8

The air had turned chilly, which was unusual for this time of year. Emir Faisal Muhammed, the second man in command of the Islamic State, Syria, and Iraq looked around his compound at his men and followers. He was restless. Several trusted colleagues sat at a table with him and shared a hookah. Faisal was the biological father of Sonia Amon, a physician and an officer in the United States Army. That fact alone galled him and burned him to his core. It angered him that she'd rejected him, not once, not twice, but hundreds of times. She'd spent her entire life rejecting him, his beliefs, and his way of life. She'd shunned him ever since she'd escaped from him at the age of eighteen.

His mind wandered back to ancient history - almost forty years ago when he was married to Melody, before Sonia was born. He remembered beating Melody and Sonia watching. He'd stupidly believed he could turn her into a Syrian woman when they'd married, but it just hadn't happened. Failure inflamed him.

Sonia. He had an intense sixth sense for her. He knew she was close by. He could sense it, feel it even. For a few moments, his memory regressed to the beautiful infant and toddler Sonia had been. He remembered her so well. He could almost feel her pudgy arms and legs and the wet kisses she gave him when they went for ice cream in the village.

He looked around the courtyard of his compound. The bunkhouse that housed fifty of his closest men was to his left. His eyes looked over at the barn, where Sonia's playroom was. It remained on the second floor, untouched for years. The years she'd been a part of his life were the happiest years of his life. Now, he hated her and loved her at the same time. Why couldn't she understand his beliefs, his philosophies, his need to destroy the West? She was a smart woman. A doctor. He passed the hookah to the man on his right. "Is there any Intel about my daughter? Do we know if she'll return to Syria?"

His confidant shrugged his shoulders, an uncertain look in his eyes. "I don't know for sure, but I have heard that she will come back soon. One of our men told me this a week or two ago."

Anger blanched Faisal's face. *She was coming back. He'd get her this time.* He hated his daughter, Sonia, his child with the American woman he'd mistakenly married so many years ago. It angered him and grated on his nerves every day that both women remained free, now living close together near the capital city of the infidels. Without him. They lived happily without him. How could that be?

"Check your source. I want her taken and brought to me so she can be tried under Sharia law."

Youssef, his friend of many years, understood Faisal's need to possess his daughter. He also knew Faisal loved her even though he swore he'd kill her. He looked into his friend's eyes and shook his head. "Are you sure that's wise? We've tried to get her before, but she is always surrounded by the strongest of American soldiers. She is heavily guarded."

Faisal gritted his teeth. "We are smarter than they are. I don't care how guarded she is. She and her mother have avoided me for years. I want them both dead before me so I can see that the task is done."

Another soldier spoke up. "I have a contact close to the American military. I have used him to plan our attack. He has two children, and he goes there often and talks with the American soldiers. I can ask him to look for a woman."

Faisal nodded. "Thank you, my brother. That is what I want to hear. I've heard it rumored that Sonia would be back to work in the clinic to help the sick children. We must check the clinic every day, and then, when she is there, we will take her."

"The clinic is closed. It has been closed for six months. Perhaps the Americans will open it back up." Youssef looked at the Emir. He knew he'd be angry.

"It's closed?" Anger crossed Faisal's face. "Why is it closed?"

"Because all of the doctors and nurses left because it wasn't safe. But, that is a good plan. We could easily take her at the clinic when it reopens."

Faisal nodded. "I agree, but only to a point. We don't have time to wait. We've got the firepower and the men to take the Army installation anytime. We will take it and destroy it in a few days. I want to make sure our new chemical lab is running well and that we are making the weapons that we need there." Faisal's eyes shone with a dark intensity.

"Good plan. Good plan." Youssef applauded. "We will do it. We will take out the American soldiers, get your daughter, and take care of anyone who defies us anywhere in this land," Youssef stood, hookah in hand amid cheers all around him.

"Let us party and be happy this evening for soon we will fight," Faisal said as he raised the hookah in the air to a rousing cheer from his men.

Chapter 9

I never thought I would see a beautiful dawn in war-torn Syria. I laid on the bed next to Paul Grayson, who I was convinced was the most handsome man in the world and the love of my life. I studied his face. The rich, pink dawn sunlight that streamed in through his window beamed on Paul's face. He had never looked more handsome than he did at this moment in the dawn of a new day in war-gutted Syria.

Paul still slept. I was able to see his little boy face in the mature face of the American Colonel whose boots were on the ground directing the war in Syria. Last night, Paul had been overjoyed to see me. He'd reached for me greedily when my transport arrived. I couldn't believe how much I'd missed him. I thought my heart was going to explode when I disembarked the plane. I'd had a few serious romances over the years, and in truth, it took me a lot to trust a man – for obvious reasons. Several guys had told me I had "daddy issues" which is probably true. But, I'd learned to trust Paul after several years, and we'd been "together" for about six years. Way long enough to plan a wedding which we planned to do when Paul retired.

I traced Paul's hairline with my index finger. I hoped he'd wake up and take me in his arms again. Instead, he flopped over and rooted deeper into his mattress. I smiled to myself and thought how absolutely exhausted he must be.

I laid in bed expecting to hear the sounds of Army life in the morning, but it was strangely quiet. A couple of minutes later, I heard a few enlisted men talking and laughing on their way to the DFAC, otherwise known as the dining facility or mess tent. Then I smelled bacon and for some reason that brought a huge grin to my face. I remembered a couple of years ago when Paul was home on leave, and I made him a bacon, lettuce, and tomato sandwich for dinner. He'd told me it was the best sandwich he'd ever eaten. I checked my watch. It was after six in the morning. I gently shook his shoulder, "Paul, Paul, you gotta get up. It's getting late. We gotta get movin'!" Paul didn't move. I shook him again. "You're the boss!"

47

Paul opened his hazel eyes and pushed his hair back on his face. His eyes warmed, and he smiled as soon as he saw me.

"Oh my God, Sonia. You look beautiful! What a wonderful surprise and a wonderful morning." He reached out, grabbed me, and held tightly.

"I've missed you so much, Paul Grayson! You've gotta retire and join me on the other side of the pond." My eyes twinkled, and my heart pumped happily. "I can't keep taking these long overnight flights to visit you." I teased. "Plus," I grinned as I looked around, "I've heard it can be dangerous over here."

Paul laughed and covered my face with kisses. "I don't see where you're on the other side of the pond. Looks to me like you're on the other side of my bed." His hungry eyes stared down at me.

I sighed contentedly as I savored his kisses. Then I shrugged my shoulders. "Seriously, I miss you so much. You know what I mean. Shoot, even my mother misses and loves you." I confided.

Paul's eyes danced. He loved my mother. "She does? How is Melody? She's the second love of my life, next to her beautiful daughter," he said as he kissed me.

"Mom's great. We had dinner last night before I left. There is no surprise when I say she's upset that I'm back over here, particularly with you know who being back in the news so much lately."

A frown crossed Paul's face. "Yeah, your father. He's around, and possibly a lot closer than we'd like to think. I guess you know he calls himself an Emir now."

I gritted my teeth with anger. "Yeah, Jeff told me that on the way over." I shook my head. "Who does he think he is... a king or something?" I sniffed and gave Paul my most disdainful look.

Paul looked into my eyes. "There's a lot of people who do consider him royalty. They also consider him high military, not to mention aristocratic. Unfortunately, believe it or not, there are thousands of people who would die for your father."

I just shook my head. "My father is a pathetic moron." I couldn't continue the conversation. After all, my father was a horrible monster. Every nation in the world had called out against him and the terrorism that he conducted in Syria and Iraq. "Let's change the subject. I'm pretty sure we're not gonna be able to fix this, and we gotta be somewhere else at 0730."

Paul's eyebrows arched. "Oh, where do we have to be?"

I shook my head. "Well, maybe not you, but I've got to meet with someone from the health minister's office about setting up some clinics to give simple immunizations while I'm here."

Paul nodded his head slowly. "That's great. These people, the good civilians around here, have suffered the torture of the damned. It'd also be good if you could set up and staff a couple of general medical clinics as well. There are lots of sick people here and 'lots of' can mean a couple of diseases."

"Yeah, that's what I've heard. Before I left the states, I attended a meeting with the WHO task force designated to clean up the public health system and general medical system here."

Paul's green eyes caught my brown ones. "You do know that we no longer have a hospital, correct? In fact, there are very few hospitals anywhere in Syria."

I stared at him and shook my head dumbly. A horrible feeling jettisoned through my body. I hadn't heard the hospital was destroyed. "The hospital is gone? What happened?" I was shocked.

Paul sat up on the side of the bunk, got up, and then moved toward his dresser. "The same thing that always happens. The terrorists. This time, we think ISIS is responsible." He shook his head as his eyes wandered around the small room.

My gut clenched. "So, tell me, Paul. What did they do to the local hospital?"

"There was a skirmish between some of the local citizens and some terrorists, specifically ISIS, we think." Paul stopped for a moment. He knew she would be upset. She'd worked with the Syrian doctors and nurses off and on.

My anxiety skyrocketed. "What, did they kill everyone?" I knew I had a wild look in my eyes. He walked over to me, sat back down on the bed, and put his arm around my shoulder.

"ISIS attacked the hospital about three months ago, shortly after you left. They were caring for some people that ISIS considered their enemy. When the hospital administrator and doctors refused to turn the two men over, the terrorists killed them. Murdered two doctors and the administrator in cold blood. Then they killed most of the patients and all of the staff that didn't run away." Paul's speech was clipped. He was still furious about the attack on innocent people.

Shock and fatigue overcame me. I felt physically ill. These bastards had killed doctors, nurses, and other staff who were taking care of their wounded. I rubbed tears from my eyes, but other tears followed, and my eyes burned with hot, unshed tears. I couldn't quiet the horrific pain that grew in my chest. I turned away from Paul, laid down on the bed, and faced the makeshift wall. My heart beat constantly and reverberated in my mind as I remembered my good friends at the local hospital in this province. Most were the best physicians and nurses I'd ever seen or worked with.

Paul sat down by my side and took my hand. He rubbed little circles on my palm. He knew that always helped de-stress me. "Who's left?" I asked in a little voice.

"Drs. Saha and Awad." He watched me carefully.

Was that all? My heart beat sluggishly, and erratically. How was I gonna set up medical clinics, two or three of them, when there were only two doctors left? Of course, it'd be okay while I was here, but when I left one clinic would be missing a physician. Perhaps I could ask Paul for a nurse practitioner or a physician assistant. That would work.

"Are all the rest of them dead?" I looked away from Paul's face. I didn't want his body language to crash my spirits before his words.

"Yes, I'm afraid most of them were killed by hostiles." He paused for a moment and then continued. "There's a young physician, a Syrian who trained with us in Iraq, and two nurses. They've traveled around and met community health needs the best they can. They haven't set up a permanent hospital, although that will be possible once we're able to push the Islamic State back further."

I laughed out loud. "You don't really believe that do you?" I'm sure my face was incredulous. "Do you really think the Americans are going to push the Islamic State out of Syria? Even though the White House has declared that America has already beat terrorism in Syria?"

Paul nodded his head slowly. "Regardless, yeah. I think we're gonna win. I don't know when or how soon but yeah, I have to believe that." He scowled at her.

I nodded. "Then I believe you," I said with a bright smile. "It's really good to hear." I reached out and hugged Paul, who hugged me in return.

He looked down at me and said, "Lazybones, you need to get back to your own quarters, get cleaned up, and meet me in the officer's mess for breakfast." He smiled. "Although, I'm fairly sure most people know that we're a couple."

I jumped up, put my hand on my waist, and tilted my head back. "Really? People know we're a couple. I haven't told anyone," I admitted as I picked up my duffel bag and gear and snuck out the back of Colonel Paul Grayson's personal quarters to my smaller living space a short distance away.

Paul shook his head and watched me slip out. "I love you; you know that Sonia, right?"

I flashed him a smile and watched his hazel eyes crinkle up. "I know. I love you too, but don't let it go to your head!" I teased as I snuck through the side of the tent. I turned back and said, "Be sure you comb that cowlick. It looks funny!"

Chapter 10

Breakfast was in full swing when I entered the mess tent. I saw Paul sitting with a couple of his officers and another group of men that I didn't know. All of them were feasting on bacon, eggs, and ham. My stomach growled at the smell of the bacon. I spied coffee and orange juice to the side, went over, and grabbed some orange juice, coffee, and a glass of milk. Then I saw Jeff sitting in the corner with another dude I didn't know. He caught my eye and waved me over.

"Good morning, Jeff." I nodded at the gentleman I didn't know.

"Major Amon, good morning. Meet Sergeant Sneed."

I turned and gave Sergeant Sneed my brightest smile. "Good morning, Sergeant what brings you to lovely Syria this time of year?"

Sneed grinned. Then he snickered. "I reckon I'm here for the same reason you are, Major. It goes something like 'let's get the bad guys.'"

I laughed out loud as I took my seat. Sergeant Sneed had happy blue eyes and wrinkles that crinkled in the corners. He was a man who'd spent most of his life smiling, and trust me, there aren't many of those living in the Middle East or in the United States Army. I turned to Jeff. "I like this guy. He's much better than most of your friends," I laughed.

Jeff nodded approvingly. "That's good, Sonia because Sergeant Sneed is gonna work side by side with you to put together a couple of healthcare clinics in the next few weeks."

I smiled from ear to ear. "Sergeant, we're gonna have fun! Now, is it just gonna be the two of us or do you have any men attached to you?"

Sneed laughed. "Major, I got the best platoon of men you'll find anywhere in this dismal, burned up, burned out dump of a country."

I gave Sergeant Sneed my most dazzling smile. "That's the best news I've heard in weeks. By chance, do you have a medic somewhere in that platoon who can check blood pressures and give injections?"

Sergeant Sneed nodded. "That I do. I got a couple of them. Jeff tells me the plane you guys came in on is filled with medical supplies. That true?"

I nodded. "It sure is. We've got tons of vaccinations, immunizations, antibiotics, and the ten most widely prescribed drugs in the United States. I feel fortunate we were able to get so many supplies together so quickly, and to be on a committee that's invested in improving the state of healthcare in Syria, particularly in this area, and also closer to Damascus." I picked up my coffee and took a sip, "We'll be able to do a lot of good."

"Did Colonel Grayson tell you we no longer have a hospital here?" I noticed the look of dismay on Jeff's face.

I nodded my head. My eyes clouded with tears. "Yeah, yes he did, and that is tragic. He also told me there are a few healthcare providers that are working on their own, providing healthcare as best they can."

Sergeant Sneed nodded. "Yeah, there are, and they're doing good work. Generally, a couple of my men go with them."

I smiled. "That's terrific. Do you have any idea where we should put these clinics, any specific locations?"

Jeff took a bite of his eggs. "I'd like to set one of them up right here on our command, maybe set a little bit apart from us, but within the perimeter. That way it'll be easy to protect the healthcare workers and the patients. But, we'll have to get permission from the Colonel."

"And I've got an idea for the second one," Sneed interjected. "It's about fifteen miles from here, but there's a couple of villages close by and there are a lot of kids that need help. There are elderly folks there too. The building won't need too much work. I've already checked it out."

I beamed my approval. "That's fantastic, Sergeant. Maybe you can take me there soon."

He nodded. "That'd be my pleasure, Major."

I turned to Jeff. "These are great ideas. If we can do that, we can possibly open three areas where we can handle patients for clinic visits."

Jeff nodded. "What about acute medical care? Are you prepared for that?"

I shook my head. "I'm afraid not. It'll have to be clinic visits for now," I reported. "We don't have the supplies we need for an acute-care facility. Perhaps we can build one soon, though. The Army has these really neat pods now that can be assembled quickly for acute care. Kind of an answer to the old mash units."

Jeff nodded. "That'll certainly be our goal. We really need some acute care here."

A deep voice startled us. "May I join you all?"

I looked up and smiled into the smiling eyes of our post commander. "Of course you can, Colonel Grayson. We'd be delighted," I gushed as I pulled out the chair next to me.

Paul nodded at Sergeant Sneed and Jeff. "It looks like you folks have been doing a lot of talking over here."

I nodded. "Yeah. We're planning a few health clinics where we can offer some general public health care, vaccinations, and limited sick care. We wondered if we could open the first one here, at the compound."

"Absolutely. We can stake it off today and possibly get part of it built using modular parts."

Sergeant Sneed smiled. "You show me where Colonel and my men and I will get to work."

"I'll do that. Let me talk with a couple of my officers, and we'll decide the most strategic spot." Paul hesitated, "Although, in the meantime, Sergeant, I want you and your men to look around and make some recommendations for me as well."

Sneed nodded. "Done." He stood up, nodded to Jeff, and saluted the Colonel. "I'm on my way, Sir."

I smiled at Sergeant Sneed. "Thank you, Sergeant. I'll catch up with you later today."

I watched Sneed leave the mess tent. "Anyone else want coffee? I'm about to get a refill and a bagel."

Jeff shook his head and stood. "Nah. I gotta get over and check on some stuff, plus I'm expecting some Intel from headquarters. I've got a few contacts I want to catch up with this morning."

Paul nodded. "Take some guys with you if you need, Jeff. We've had trouble this week on a couple of patrols. There were some insurgents hiding out and jumping people. We've had a couple of hostiles around. I'm sending out three patrols today." He paused and replaced his coffee mug on the table. "I just learned this morning that terrorists killed a young family about seven miles south of here. A mother, a grandmother, and two children." He shook his head.

"Rebels?" Jeff looked down at Paul and me.

Paul shook his head. "No. I don't think so. No indication they were, based on the information I got. Just women and children."

"These people are chickens." *Bastards. I hated these extremists.* I wondered if Paul and Jeff hated these people as much as I did. Sometimes, on some level, I think I'm responsible since my monster father pretty much runs this part of Syria. I'd never tell that to an Army psychiatrist. Between that and my "daddy issues," I'd never get out of therapy. I grinned to myself. On second thought, maybe I would. I could only imagine the looks on the shrink's face.

Jeff nodded. "No argument from me, Major." He turned to Paul, "Appreciate the offer for protection, Colonel, but I'm gonna go it alone. It'd freak my contacts if I showed up with a platoon of the United States Army's finest."

The Colonel nodded. "Understood. Use your judgment. We've got resources if you need them."

"Understood, Sir. On another subject, when should we go out to the bombed-out building? Sonia wants to go through the rubble, run some tests."

I nodded. "Yeah, and I'll need space for a small laboratory, Colonel."

Paul smiled at me. "You want to go through some burned out buildings, Sonia? We can arrange that."

"Yeah. Reid Handley told me where to look. I'd like to check it out before too much more time goes by. I promised him I'd get back to him soon."

Paul's face sobered. "How's Reid? You must have seen him. He was pretty beat up when we lifted him out of here."

I paused. "He's bad, Paul. And frankly, Sir, I don't know how much time Reid has. His radiation lab work hadn't come back before I left, but he had acute radiation poisoning." I tried to keep my voice clear and even, but I knew I'd faltered.

Paul shook his head. "Sorry to hear that, Sonia." He squeezed my hand under the table. "How about this afternoon? It's just a few miles down the road." He looked up at Jeff. "Does that work for you?"

Jeff nodded. "Yeah. How about mid-afternoon?"

Colonel Grayson nodded. "Good. I wanted to take Dr. Amon to visit a couple of my men in our makeshift medical unit here on the post. I'm sure one has a bad wound infection from shrapnel."

"Sounds good. I'll meet you all back here about two o'clock this afternoon, and we'll head over to the chemical site."

Paul nodded and looked at me. "Is that okay with you, Sonia?"

"Sure. Let me go see these patients now, Colonel. I'm really not that hungry."

Jeff raised his index finger. "I'm gone, folks. I'll catch you later."

I waved bye to Jeff and stood to leave the mess tent. "Let's go," my eyes beckoned to Paul.

He shook his head as he looked at his phone. "Let's wait about an hour. The soldier on duty said they just fell asleep. Let's let them rest before you go in there and check them out."

"Okay. Then, I'm going to grab some food."

"I'll be right here when you get back." Paul winked at me, and my heart raced. Boy, I loved that man.

I could feel his eyes on me as I poured my coffee and buttered my bagel. I dished up a scoop of eggs and grits. It was scary to love someone as much as I loved Colonel Paul Grayson. I'd learned to savor in the good times and be grateful every night when we found we were both still alive.

Chapter 11

Melody rose early the next morning. It was Saturday, and she already missed Sonia. They usually hung out together on Saturdays after she saw patients at Walter Reed. Their life had been so difficult because of her relationship with Faisal and his kidnapping of Sonia. They had each other now, and she treasured their time together.

She sat at her kitchen table where she drank her coffee every morning. She pushed back her long blonde hair and continued to reminisce about the peaks and valleys of her life. Her thoughts returned to her escape from Aleppo. She wondered about the two old Syrian women and the village elder who'd provided her money and tickets for Sonia and her to escape. Did these women know how horrible Faisal would become? Had they seen the writing on the wall? Where had two elderly women gotten the money? She figured the CIA had intervened with the blessing of her illustrious, wealthy father, but she'd never known for sure.

She reached for the coffee pot and refilled her cup. She loved coffee and used a French Press. She savored the rich, dark taste of the brew as she considered her plans for the day. She knew she'd get a message from Sonia telling her all was well, but she felt uneasy. Fear sat in her belly like a loaded rifle. *Why am I so scared? Sonia has spent years in Syria, and she's never been captured. Why am I so concerned this time?* Deep down inside, she knew Faisal was getting old and was more desperate which was most likely why he wanted to get Sonia.

Melody continued to analyze her situation for a couple more minutes and decided she needed to get herself together and do her grocery shopping. She decided to try the new Aldi's market that wasn't far from her home. She'd heard they had great fruit and excellent produce. She'd become a vegetarian of sorts in recent years. She smiled when her telephone rang. She knew that it was her beloved daughter.

"Are you there, darling?" she asked in a breathless voice.

"I am, Mom. It's the same here except maybe a little bit worse. Everything is so bleak and burned out." I sighed. "If truth be known, it's actually pretty depressing."

Melody was concerned about her daughter's mood. Sonia was generally upbeat about everything she did. "Well, honey, I don't think you'll have time to rebuild Syria in two or three weeks."

"Yeah, that's true, but at least I can build a couple of medical clinics to help American servicemen and the Syrian people. It's just pathetic here. It truly is."

"I'm so sorry to hear that, Sonia." She changed the subject. "But, how is that handsome Colonel Paul Grayson? Is he as good-looking as ever?" Melody's voice had a smile in it.

My mood changed, and I was immediately happy. "Yes, he's just as wonderful as ever. He's very busy, as his command here has grown, and I suspect it will continue to grow. We had breakfast together and plan to have dinner together every day." My heart felt light and my spirit soared.

Melody smiled. She was so happy for her daughter. She truly believed that Paul was the perfect man for Sonia. She'd met him several times and liked him very much. He allowed Sonia to be herself and pursue her dreams. "I'm so glad to hear that. Please give him my love. When will he retire?"

"He's got a few more months. Plus, as you know, he's kind of like me, so the chances are pretty good we'll both be back and forth to the Middle East until we're old and feeble."

"Yeah, I suppose so." Melody's voice was wistful. "I understand you have a job to do, and I know you have the interest of Syria in your blood. You'd have to." My mother didn't sound happy about it, but at least she acknowledged my reality.

"I suppose I do. Truthfully, I want to help the villagers and the refugees. Not just here, but all over the Middle East. I'm looking forward to being part of the group that oversees world healthcare for these poor people whose lives have been turned upside down for years." As soon as the words had left my mouth, I was sorry.

That was the last thing Melody wanted to hear. In her mind, she had been robbed of her daughter for many years when she was held by her father outside Aleppo. She truthfully didn't want to share her anymore. Of course, there was nothing she could do. It was her daughter's passion – medicine and the Middle

East. "I suppose you'll always have half your heart in Syria." Melody's voice was despondent.

I picked up on her sadness. "Your voice sounds sad. I'm sorry, Mom. It's just who I am." Sonia paused. "What are your plans for the day? Are you going shopping?"

Melody laughed. "I only go shopping with you so you can tell me what to buy, but I am going out to get groceries. I'll probably rent a couple movies. I want to see *Rhapsody in Blue*."

"That sounds terrific. Just realize that when I get back, we're gonna rent it again because I want to see it too." I was happy my mother had planned her evening entertainment.

"That sounds like a plan. I'll put it on my calendar," Melody promised.

"I guess I'd better go. I want to get over to my little office and lab and do a little research. I'll call you tomorrow or the next day."

"You'd better, or I'll beat you when you get home," Melody teased.

A few seconds later, Melody picked up her purse and her grocery list and went from the kitchen into her one car garage.

She never made it to her car. Strong arms grabbed her and stuck a rag in her mouth. A couple of minutes later, her car left the garage. The driver was a dark-haired man with a beard.

Chapter 12

F aiz stood in the shadow of a burned out building in Aleppo. He checked his watch for the third time in as many minutes and took a quick walk through the blackened ruins to see if his contact was inside. The building was empty. Faiz closed his eyes and remembered the Aleppo of only five years ago. It had been a booming city and the oldest continuously occupied in the world filled with history, museums, and beauty. Now, the hammams, souqs, and basilicas were reduced to rubble. Tons of barrel bombs dropped from helicopters had destroyed the beautiful city.

He'd read where the destruction of his homeland and city was described as the deadliest conflicts of the twenty-first century. It was the worst thing he'd ever experienced. Over three hundred thousand of his countrymen were killed in the armed conflict that used bombs, bullets, chemical attacks, and airstrikes to destroy what was once called the cradle of civilization. The conflict began when Syrians protested government policies and escalated into a full-scale civil war against President Bashar Assad's regime that was fueled by Russian artillery and money.

Faiz was a former member of the Syrian army and now a rebel. Tears streamed down his face as he tried to remember where buildings had been as he looked up and down block after block after block of rubble that used to be his home. Faiz had lived in the east end of Aleppo, which had been a rebel stronghold since 2012. He'd fought hard to destroy the government forces and their Russian allies. Faiz wiped tears from his eyes. His heart was still broken six years later. He missed his home and dead relatives and friends. The rebels that had escaped had reestablished themselves and were growing in number. One day, they would be victorious over Assad and the Islamic State. They'd turn back their traitor President and the murderous Emir Faisal Muhammed. Syrians would glory in the day when it came.

He turned to the sound of footsteps. He recognized his American friend and quickly walked toward him. The two men hugged to show their support and friendship for each other. The pair went back over twenty years.

Jeff broke the hug and looked into Faiz's eyes. "How goes it, my friend? Are you doing well?"

Faiz smiled. "Yes, many of us have gathered and once again have formed a group of rebels. Our army is growing again. Our camp is south of here. We hope to be active soon, but, as you can tell, the landscape has changed."

Jeff put his arm around Faiz's shoulder. The two men walked toward a pile of rubble where they sat down.

"You look good my friend," Jeff said, "What do you mean when you say the landscape has changed?"

Faiz's eyes looked away from Jeff and toward the mountain. "We have more and more members of the Islamic State coming here every week. Soon, we will be overrun," he said, a dark look on his face. "Your president has not defeated ISIS no matter what he says. Yes, the Americans have pushed them back and back, but they're not defeated."

Jeff nodded. "Yes. We know that. I don't think our troops will be leaving. I think that's just bureaucratic bull talk. Don't worry."

"Bureaucratic or not, it's given ISIS the leverage they need to come back this way and rebuild." Faiz's voice was bitter, hostile. His dark eyes had a look of desperation.

Jeff shook his head. "I'm sorry about that. The head of my agency knows better, and we are in conversation with the White House every day. Hopefully, we will get all of that remedied soon."

Relief filtered over Faiz's face. "I'm so relieved to hear that. Any idea when?"

Anxiety shot through Jeff. "I don't have a date, but I suspect soon," he said as he looked into his friend's eyes. Faiz grasped his hand. "Thank you, man. Thank you. I know you don't always hear this, but the Syrian people are grateful for you and your country. The Americans have saved us, at least those who are left. I am thankful for your country every single day," he swore and smiled. "I promise you, we are."

Jeff nodded. "Do you have any info for me about the Emir? And the other stuff we talked about?"

A look of disgust crossed Faiz's face at the mention of the Emir. "Faisal is here. As a matter-of-fact, he's close by, at his home up the road. He knows his daughter is at the Army garrison." Faiz's eyes bored into Jeff's. "I'm sure you know what that means."

Anger and bewilderment crossed Jeff's face. "How in the hell did he find out she was here? We just got here last night. Plus, we only planned this trip a couple of days ago." Jeff was stunned. He cursed under his breath as he tried to remember who knew he'd whisked Sonia off on an overnight flight to Syria. The only ones he could remember were his immediate superior and Sonia's mother.

Faiz shook his head. "I have no idea, man, but the Emir and his men know everything. And you know how dangerous they are."

Jeff nodded. He didn't need to be reminded. "Yeah. Anything else? Do you know how he plans to grab her?"

Faiz shook his head and pressed his lips together. "No. I don't, but I do know he's determined. He knows her trips to Syria will occur less and less often now that she is no longer active Army. I imagine he's more determined than ever. He also plans to go after the Major's mother."

Melody. After all these years? Fear, mingled with anger, jumped up and down Jeff's spine. He shrugged his shoulders. "He wants Melody too?" He shook his head and kicked a rock down the road. "Something has rekindled his anger, or someone must have angered him. Melody has been out of witness protection for several years. Why does he want her now?"

Faiz shrugged his shoulders. "I don't know what to say. I can only tell you what I hear from others. This information came to me early this morning from one of his most trusted colleagues."

Jeff's mind wandered as he whittled down the short list of his trusted colleagues who could have ratted on Sonia Amon's whereabouts. "I see. I trust the information implicitly, Faiz. Is there anything else on Sonia or can I change the subject?"

Faiz shook his head. "No. That's all I know. There is nothing else on that matter. I do think he'll take her as soon as he can. He's at his home a short distance away, maybe fifteen or twenty miles. What else do you need?"

"Major, or Dr. Amon as she is known now, and I are here on orders to open several medical centers. One, of course, will be at the Army compound. The other clinic will be for the Syrian people. Any suggestions for a location?"

Faiz's eyes shone with gratitude. "Thank you so much. There are so many of us who need medical help now. Rebels, solid Syrian men, and villagers need clean dressings. We are also in need of antibiotics for our battle wounds. Our children are sick and need care. We will accept any and all the help you can provide." He gave Jeff a grateful smile.

Jeff touched Faiz on his shoulder. "I'm sure Sonia will be happy to visit you and give them care. We brought a plane full of medical supplies. You will have what you need, and we will help your men as well."

Faiz was so thankful that tears slid down his face. "Thank you, Jeff. Thank you from the bottom of my heart."

Jeff prodded him. "Now, show me where she should put the clinic. It will be temporary, but it needs to be in a safe area while she is here. She plans to see children and adults. She hopes to give the children their immunizations."

"I think the safest place would be close to where we're camped. Many Syrian citizens come there for help every day anyway. That way, we can offer her some protection, and some of the women can help with the children."

Jeff nodded. "That sounds good. How far is that from the Army post? How many kilometers?"

Faiz scratched his beard. "About ten or so. It's near the market the Emir destroyed last year. He burned it down. The market is back in business now. When the locals get food to sell, that can also be a diversion if we need one."

Jeff nodded. "Sounds good to me. Let me run it by Colonel Grayson. He has the last word. We also have some protection as well. Sergeant Sneed's people will be part of the Major's protection detail."

Faiz nodded and checked his watch. "I must go. I will check with my contact in the Emirs camp for more Intel, and I'll contact you the same way."

Jeff nodded. "That's good. Same place?"

Faiz looked past him down the road. He motioned for Jeff to move further into the building. "Yeah. Be very careful here, Jeff. Tell the Colonel that more ISIS fighters are pouring in each day. The Emir has plans for something, and I think it's something big."

Jeff cursed under his breath. He'd known in his gut that something was up. "Any idea what he plans?"

Faiz shook his head. "Not at this point, but the building the terrorists sleep in at his home compound is full. He has taken on more personal bodyguards."

Jeff frowned. "Yeah. This does sound conclusive. I'll need to notify Colonel Grayson. He may need more troops, maybe three or four platoons." Jeff's mind exploded with the possible scenarios Faisal could be planning.

Faiz nodded. "Based on history, when Faisal reinforces troops like this, he has plans for a disastrous event. He's pulling in warriors from Iraq daily."

Jeff nodded as uncertainty crawled up his back. He tried to keep his face non-committal. "Thanks, man. Keep in touch. If nothing else pops, I'll see you in a couple of days."

Faiz watched as Jeff slipped out of the building. He walked in the shadow of the wall until he was out of sight. He shook his head. He had a bad feeling about the relationship with the Americans and the Emir. He sighed deeply. He was pretty sure something was up with Faisal. His intuition convinced him that the relationship between the Emir and the American military had worsened. He believed what his gut told him. He shook off the bad feeling.

Faiz's mind wandered. He thought about Sonia, the Emir's daughter. He remembered her from when she was a baby. He also remembered her beautiful mother with the long blonde hair who had been so sweet to him at Faisal's home years ago. He knew Sonia would never remember him, but they had played together when they were children. He was five years older but remembered the times they'd played marbles. Several times, he'd heard her crying in her father's walled garden. It wasn't clear what had happened to the Emir's beautiful American wife, but he knew she'd disappeared. He also knew that Faisal had beaten her severely. He used to see Melody at the market. He often waited and watched her and asked her if he could carry her bag back home. He'd thought the American woman was exquisite. He'd been fascinated by her looks – her pale skin and her long blonde curls. Later, he became enamored by her voice and her sweetness of spirit. He was always happy around Melody. He'd experienced the joy that flowed from her. He'd never seen anyone play and laugh like Sonia's mother. But, that was in the early days.

One day when he waited for her at the market, he noticed she carried her market sack in a different hand. He'd asked Melody if he could carry her package for her. She smiled at him and handed it over. The three of them, the American with two children, shopped side-by-side. It wasn't until they were finished shopping and she reached for money to pay that he noticed her wrist was crooked and seemed pushed to one side. As he looked back, he now knew the Emir had broken her wrist. He'd also seen signs of bruises when her burqa had fallen back and exposed her full face. One of her blue eyes was blood red. He was furious that her husband had hurt her so badly, but he was powerless to do anything about it. He was just a child. One day, he knew that would change.

Faiz's heart burned with hate whenever he thought of Sonia's father. His father had been part of Faisal's tribe for years and had been a loyalist to the Emir's family. But he knew the Emir was a cruel coward and a brute. In the twelve years he'd lived on Faisal's land, he'd seen things done to men that should never be done to anyone - not to any creature that roamed the earth. He knew in his heart he could never work for such a man.

His thoughts returned to Sonia. He remembered her dancing around the courtyard with her mother. Her long coppery curls had shone in the sunlight, and her little feet had danced all the way across the marbled area. He'd watched from a distance and at the age of seven years, had fallen in love with the tiny little girl. One day, a couple of local musicians were playing their instruments as Melody and Sonia danced. Faisal had been infuriated the other men had watched his wife dance and play with his daughter. Faisal had moved angrily across the marbled pathway, grabbed Melody's arm, and twisted it. He remembered the fear on Melody's face. She turned white as her husband berated her in front of the other men and women of the village. A moment later, he had slapped her so hard that she'd fallen to the ground. Sonia ran to her mother's crumpled form and laid down, kissing her face. Her mother hugged the little girl close until her father ordered his men to pull the screaming child away from her mother.

Faiz learned later that Faisal had jailed Melody for three days without food or water. He saw her the day after she was released, but the beautiful young woman was never the same. She never smiled and always appeared nervous, anxious, or frightened. Her mood passed to her daughter as well, and Sonia became withdrawn and anxious. He never saw the mother and daughter dance together again, and their playtime was their journey to the village market for vegetables. Melody and Sonia never spoke aloud in public or around any men or women that could be attached to Faisal.

Faiz watched Melody and Sonia each day when they went to the market. About five months after the attack in the courtyard, he saw a stranger, a woman, pass Melody a package at the market which she quickly hid under her robes.

Two weeks later, Melody and Sonia disappeared. Somehow, in the dead of night, the woman and her child had escaped the Emir's men and reached Aleppo where they flew to the United States.

Faisal was furious his wife had left him and taken his beloved daughter. He raged for days and vowed to kill his wife and find his daughter.

Faiz joined the Syrian Army a few years later. He gradually became disillusioned with the government and their cruelty toward the citizens of Syria. He'd left the Army, made his way back to his hometown, and joined the resistance. He was a rebel.

He'd never been sorry, not one day in his life. His desire to destroy Emir Faisal Muhammed was greater now than it had ever been.

Chapter 13

Jeff found me at a table in the DFAC, the mess tent. I had a list of medical supplies in front of me and was ordering more. A tuna sandwich, also sat in front of me, with only one bite missing.

"How was your morning?" I smiled and waved him over when he entered the tent.

"It was pretty good. I caught up with my contact." Jeff flashed me a smile. *Sonia looks great in her army fatigues,* he thought, *with her hair pulled back, and her eyes shining with excitement.*

"Looks like you got some info for us." My stomach tightened.

Jeff nodded and looked at the floor. He shifted from one foot to the other. "Yeah. I'll tell you in a little bit."

"Where'd you meet him?"

"Aleppo. I drove part of the way, stashed my vehicle, and then walked to the old market near the town." He shook his head sadly. "It still breaks my heart when I look at the devastation there. It was such a beautiful city," he noted as he placed his phone and vehicle keys on the table. "How's the tuna? I think I'm gonna grab an iced tea. Would you like one?"

"Tuna's pretty good – if you like tuna. Tea sounds good. The coffee tastes bad. And, I agree about Aleppo. I prefer to remember it as the beautiful, gilded city it was. I can remember my parent's taking me there to shop and dine when I was little. We'd sit in the park and eat ice cream. It was so beautiful back then... the temples, the buildings." I choked back a sob. "Those are probably the only good memories I have of my parents together.

"Well, keep them in your heart because it doesn't look to me like there is any attempt to rebuild the city."

"Go get your lunch. Paul should be here soon. He's got a couple of wounded men that need a special kind of wound dressing for their shrapnel wounds. I'm hoping we can get them here soon. In the meantime, I've packed and debrided their wounds. I also taught the medics how to do it as well. Do you know of any planes coming in soon?"

"Should be one on Monday afternoon. Let me know what you need, and I'll ask that it be placed on that plane."

I grinned. "You're the man to know, Jeff Hansen. You've got the keys to all the treasure in this hell hole."

Jeff laughed shortly. "Yeah. Lucky, lucky me. Let me know if there's anything else by late this evening."

I watched Jeff as he headed toward the food area. He was a good man. He'd saved my life more than once, and I had a sneaky suspicion that he was about to do it again. I knew very little about Jeff personally. We'd worked together for years, and he was one of the few people who knew Faisal was my father. Over the years, particularly since he was part of the Middle East desk, Jeff had built a respectable number of informants and allies that were deeply involved within the extremist groups. He had large numbers of resources and informants. Several of them traveled with Faisal. He also had similar contacts in Hamas, Al Qaeda, and throughout the Islamic State, better known as ISIS. He looked Middle Eastern and spoke Farsi better than I do. We both have a good command of local languages, dialects, and cultural traditions. In truth, I was lucky to have him as my handler.

I felt a hand on my shoulder. I looked up, and it was Paul. He smiled, "I see you're still working."

I smiled as I looked up at him. He was so handsome with his light brown hair, hazel eyes, and aristocratic nose. My heart picked up a beat. "I am. I need some more medical supplies. Jeff thinks he can get them here in a couple of days. I want some different antibiotics for the guys I saw this morning, something stronger. I think they've become immune to the ones they're currently prescribed."

"Is Hansen back?"

I nodded. "Yep. He's over there grabbing lunch." I pointed at Jeff's back. "He saw a contact this morning. I think he has information for us that probably isn't good," I blurted out as a flicker of fear crossed my face.

Paul grimaced. "That's probably true. I've heard the Islamic State is sending in more fighters. At least, that's what our Intel told us this morning." He paused. "Let me grab some lunch so we can hit the road. We can talk over lunch."

I walked over with Paul to select some dessert. I watched him and Jeff load their plates with food. I had to admit the meatloaf looked pretty good. Of course, meatloaf, creamed potatoes, and green peas was my favorite meal. I was tempted to get some but decided to stick with my sandwich and chips. I'd load some carbs at dinner.

Jeff was at the table when I returned with my lemon pie. "How's the meatloaf?"

He smiled. "Pretty darn good. Wanna bite?" He held out his fork.

I shook my head but admitted I might have it for dinner.

Jeff moved his knapsack to make room for Paul.

Paul nodded at my handler. "Thanks, man. Did you learn anything this morning?"

"Yeah, more than I wanted to hear," Jeff admitted as he moved his peas around on his plate. "I hear more and more fighters are coming in, particularly since the U.S. has announced that we'll be leaving."

Paul cursed under his breath. "Yeah, wasn't that just great to hear," he smirked, his voice sarcastic. "But, I'm pretty sure no one is going anywhere."

Jeff nodded. "Well, regardless, my contact tells me more fighters are on their way and that ISIS is planning something pretty big. He's not sure what, but it's big, and he thinks it'll happen soon."

My stomach tightened with stress. I wondered if my father knew I was in Syria. I wondered if that was the motivation for bringing in more men. I shivered involuntarily and wiped chill bumps from my arms.

"Are you cold, Sonia? I have a windbreaker in my pack here," Jeff said as he reached for it. "It'll warm you right up."

"Nah. I'm okay. It just feels damp and cold in here to me. What else did you learn?"

Jeff flashed a dark look at Colonel Grayson. "Listen up, Paul. You need to hear this."

"I've been listening," Grayson assured him as he continued to attack his meatloaf. "I heard the exact same thing this morning from our Intel. They've spotted trucks moving in from the south and the north with supplies and men. They're definitely planning something... we just don't know what yet." Paul glowered as he reached for his roll and buttered it.

"I think they're possibly planning some type of chemical attack. Last week, they tested some type of chemical or germ warfare – that's what we're gonna investigate this afternoon. From what ya'll said, they killed a bunch of civilians, so they know it works." The thoughts of chemical weapons terrified me. I hoped my voice didn't shake as badly as I think it did.

Jeff nodded. "Yeah. I think you're on target. But a chemical attack doesn't necessarily demand a troop build-up. I'm wondering if they have several things in mind." Jeff scratched his beard as he contemplated the situation.

Grayson nodded his head. "Yeah. That's the fear. I've got three patrols out now going through a couple of buildings looking for anything new or different. I've also got a couple more locals we can lean on for Intel." He pushed his plate away and stood. "I'm gonna arrange for a platoon to accompany us this afternoon. No sense us walking into something we don't have to."

Jeff nodded. "That's a good idea, Paul. No telling what's out there these days."

Grayson nodded, his face grim. "I'm also putting the garrison on high alert."

My blood pressure skyrocketed. "I guess that's a good idea," I agreed in a quiet voice.

Paul nodded. "Jeff, can you meet me near the vehicle building in thirty minutes? I'm gonna have the men gas up trucks for us. We'll leave from there. We'll have full body armor and HAZMAT suits."

"Sure thing, Colonel. We'll be there," Jeff assured him.

I stared at my half-eaten sandwich. I was overcome with anxiety and dismay. Generally, I handled situations like this well, but for some reason, I was paralyzed. I realized I'd been afraid ever since I'd arrived.

"Sonia, are you okay? You look like you're out of it, in a fog bank." Jeff touched my hand. His look was one of concern.

I shook my head and climbed up from the deep abyss where I'd fallen. "I'm okay, just nervous, I guess. I hate never knowing for sure what the hell is gonna happen," I said honestly.

Jeff laughed. "Welcome to the Army! We never know much," he quipped. "We always operate on less than half of what we should know."

I grinned at him. "Yeah. I know. I'm all right. What do you want me to do?"

"Go to your quarters and put on full body armor. I don't wanna take any chances when we leave this afternoon. This place is crawling with hostiles and…" A dark look crossed his face.

"And what? What else."

Jeff shook his head. "Your old man. He's not far away, and he knows you're here. There's a lot of talk that he's gunning for you. There are gonna be a lot of people looking for you in the next few weeks, Sonia."

I almost passed out when I heard this. "How? How does he know I'm here? Who would have told him? We didn't know I was coming until a couple of days ago." I was frantic with fear and numb with disbelief. *How in the hell did that bastard know where I was?*

Paul picked up his keys and put them in his pocket. "Come on. I'm walking you to your quarters. Full-body armor and HAZMAT, okay?"

I nodded. I didn't even notice the sun had gone in the clouds or that the temperature had dropped about twenty degrees. I felt like a deaf, paralyzed mute. *I didn't want to do this. I didn't want to be in Syria.*

Chapter 14

The short trip to the burned-out building took forever. The road was a mess and deeply rutted. It had been a while since I'd ridden in an army vehicle over rough terrain. I bit my tongue twice when we hit ruts in the road. I had a heck of a time controlling the blood, but fortunately, thanks to a pack of gauze four by four's, I managed to stop it before anyone noticed. For the rest of the trip, I kept my teeth clenched.

We had a platoon with us that was commanded by Sergeant Sneed. I'd talked to him earlier and noticed him primarily because he had a hearty laugh and he laughed a lot. He had deep laugh lines around his eyes, and his men respected him. I liked the Sergeant a lot.

There was a general feeling of unrest among everyone. I noted how the soldiers kept their eyes peeled for anything they might see in the dry, barren surroundings.

I sat in the backseat with Colonel Grayson and his second Lieutenant. Jeff and another guy, one of our dog handlers, sat up front.

I was glad we'd decided to take the dogs. I missed Tessa dreadfully and wished I'd brought her with me. I knew she'd be happy with my dog sitter, but my heart ached for her. She was getting old, and I'd noticed toward the end of my last tour that she was skittish in combat areas.

Paul reached for my hand. "What are you thinking, Sonia?"

I smiled. "I was thinking how much I miss Tessa. I'd thought about bringing her, but she's getting a bit old for combat."

Paul nodded. "Yeah. She probably is, but she's a great dog. I know you miss her." He paused, "But I think it's best to leave her back in the US now the way things are here."

I nodded and held back tears. I missed everything about the United States. Even the weekday traffic I encountered on my way to and from the Army War College. "I do miss her. Tessa and I are inseparable," I admitted and changed the subject. "I brought samples of several poisons I hope the dogs will be able to sniff out. I hope it tells us what happened. First and foremost, I want to know if these people are playing with poison gas or weaponizing some horrible substance."

Paul nodded. He gritted his teeth. "Yeah, we'd all like to know that."

We arrived ten minutes later. The building structure had been reduced to rubble. I think, at one point in time, it'd been a three-story building of some type, but now only one and a half stories remained. Paul said it had been some type of school years ago. Piles of rock and debris made walking difficult, and the pieces of concrete were difficult to maneuver. *So, this was the place Reid Handley had almost met the grim reaper.* I looked around. I could still smell the smoke. I almost smelled fear and death.

Assad's men had bombed the building a few years back when rebel forces used it as a storehouse. Our troops had gone through the old building last year, but last week, Colonel Grayson had sent a patrol in for routine surveillance and encountered a dirty bomb, an RDD. The platoon had been attacked and Lieutenant Reid Handley been critically injured. Several of his men were killed.

We parked the trucks about a kilometer away from the buildings and put on HAZMAT gear. The last thing I wanted to see was any more radiation poisoning suffered by members of Paul's command – or anyone for that matter.

I waited with Jeff and Paul as the Sergeant, the dogs, and his men cleared the building. Once we knew the building was safe, our work began. Sergeant Sneed exited the rear of the building and came over to our truck. He removed his HAZMAT hood and spoke.

"It's safe to go in, Colonel, but watch where you step. There's all kinds of metal debris and rubble in all the rooms." He looked at me. "Major, it looks to me like the last room on the right is where they had chemicals stored. If we get lucky, maybe we can piece together what was in the big containers." He paused and continued. "I've ordered my men to gather as much information off the labels that they can, and they'll photograph the labels too."

I nodded. "Thank you, Sergeant Sneed. I'll head back there in a few minutes. I'd like to know what was stored here and we really need to know how they killed the civilians."

Sergeant Sneed grinned and nodded. "Yes, ma'am, we sure do. Just let me know what you need from me and my men."

I smiled and assured him I would as I jumped out of the truck. I reached over and grabbed an evidence bag. I pulled my long hair up into a ponytail and put on my HAZMAT gear.

"Okay, gentlemen, let's hit it." I looked at the men around me. "What are we waiting for?"

Sergeant Sneed grinned at me. "Nothing, Major. Nothing at all. Let's hit it."

The inside of the building was dark and smoky, plus it had a smell I vaguely recognized. Walking was treacherous because of the uneven floors and debris everywhere. Even with my HAZMAT hood, I knew there was an odor. I remembered what Lieutenant Handley had said about broken glass and lab equipment. He was right. It was all here. I picked up pieces of equipment and placed them in my knapsack as I worked my way through the building. It took me an hour to get through all the rooms. Even though I knew it was a foolish thing to do, I removed my HAZMAT hood several times, and tried to identify the smell. I gathered a lot of empty bottles with trace elements of substance in them. I hoped I could send the bottles back for analysis to find out what substances they were using. I had very limited laboratory equipment with me. I also had a limited background on how to analyze the substrates. I needed help and a fully equipped lab.

I exited the back of the building and saw Jeff and Paul a short distance away talking with a group of locals.

Paul waved. "What did you find? Anything significant?"

I shrugged my shoulders. "I'm sure I did, but honestly, I'm gonna need to send these samples to a lab and get them tested. I'm not gonna be able to identify the leftover chemicals in these bottles without outside help."

"Let's take a short walk over to the mass grave. The Sergeant has his men spread out to protect us in case anyone decides to come down this lonely country road." Jeff grinned at me.

I was happy to have the platoon of men. The sun had almost set, and dusk was moving in. I'd forgotten how scary that felt in a hostile country. I felt chill bumps pop out on my arms under my body armor and protective clothing.

I nodded and Jeff, Paul, and I walked toward the site.

"Here we are," Jeff said, his face grim. He turned to Paul. "How many civilians were killed? What was your estimate?"

"My men figured about seventy older men, women, and children. We believe ISIS took them from a mosque about twelve miles away." He shuffled his feet and kicked a rock, his handsome face contorted with anger. "At least, that's our best guess at this point." Paul looked down at the grave.

The mass grave sickened me. I was enraged. What kind of man snatches elders, women, and children from a house of worship and then kills them as an experiment. Suddenly, I felt dizzy, woozy even. I must've been ready to faint, but Paul grabbed me before I hit the ground. He hollered for a medic, and an enlisted man appeared with a first-aid kit. Jeff snatched the smelling salts and held them close to my nose. I immediately came out of it and set up my arm, pushing Jeff's hand away.

"Stop it, stop it! That burns my eyes and my throat," I hollered. "Put it away! I'm okay." I tried to stand but was dizzy and unstable. *What has happened to me? Was it fear, anger, or had I inhaled something in that building?* For a moment, I thought I'd be sick. My stomach wanted to empty into my mouth. I walked over to an area by myself in case I had to throw up. I didn't need an audience for that. Fortunately, a light evening breeze restored me, and my stomach recovered.

Paul followed me, but I waved him away. "I'm okay. Just give me a couple of minutes."

Paul and Jeff patiently waited. Both carefully watched me. I could feel the hole they stared into my back.

I wiped sweat from my forehead and unbuttoned my camo jacket. I was so hot. I felt like I was burning up. Then I walked over and sat on a rock until my head cleared. Something was wrong with me. Why had I almost passed out? Did I inhale something in that building that made me sick? Once again, that possibility ran through my mind. A barrage of questions and possibilities jammed my mind until I was hardly able to think it all.

"Are you all right, Sonia? Do you think you're able to travel back?" Paul's face was concerned, his hazel eyes anxious. He berated himself. He knew he should never have allowed Sonia back into Syria. Her enemy was so close he could smell him. But the Army and the United States government valued Sonia's skill set. Her medical training, her background in biological weapons, her appearance, and her language expertise defined her as the perfect covert operative. She could move in and out of villages and talk with locals from many tribes all over in Syria. She had excellent command of all the language dialects in Syria. She could blend in just about anywhere. She was a CIA dream operative in a hostile, unstable country riddled by war and disease.

I stood. I was still unsteady and woozy. I took a few deep breaths.

"You okay, Major?" Colonel Grayson walked toward me.

I nodded. "Yeah. I think so. Something in that building got to me, I just don't know what," I admitted. Paul was upset. I gave him a wink. "I'm okay. I promise." My voice was soft as I tried to convince him.

He stood in front of me. His voice was low. "I love you, Sonia. Are you sure you don't need medical help?"

I shook my head and offered a brief smile. "I'll be fine. Just give me a couple of minutes."

Jeff caught up with us. He checked me out from head to foot. "You're pale. Did you take off your HAZMAT gear? Your hood? Did you use the respirator the entire time?" He moved closer and stared me in the eye. "Answer me, Sonia, now." His look was stern.

A bad feeling overwhelmed me. Jeff always caught me. He knew me like a book. I nodded. "Yeah. I did take my hood off, but only for a few minutes. There was a smell in there I wanted to identify. I know that smell, but I just couldn't place it. I still can't," I admitted.

Paul glared at me and shook his head. I saw anger flash across his face, and it made me angry. "Sonia, you know better than that," he chided. "God knows what they've mixed or made in that building." The color drained from his face. "And now, you've breathed it in."

A flush crawled up my face. My face turned crimson. I held my anger. "We have to find out what killed a bunch of helpless, innocent Syrian civilians." I spat the words; my anger was palpable. "I can take care of myself, Paul. I'm not taking outrageous chances." I took a deep breathe, turned around, and pranced off leaving Paul in the dust. I hated to be reprimanded by anyone, much less Paul.

Jeff touched my waist and steered me toward our truck. "Calm down, Sonia before we get thrown out of here. It's never good to antagonize the boss."

I laughed at him and winked. "You know I hate being told what to do. I don't care who it is."

Jeff rolled his eyes and groaned. "Let's get the hell out of here. I don't like being out after dark in ISIS country."

I laughed. "Neither do I. Besides, I'm hungry."

Paul caught up and smiled at me. He reached for my arm. I could feel his forgiveness, but I was still mad and ignored him.

The three of us were headed toward our truck when an ancient rusted-out car barreled down the road near us and threw something out of the window.

It was a grenade.

The shout "GRENADE" pierced the air and all of us dove for cover. I wrapped my arms around my head. Paul threw his body over mine and Jeff was on my side closest to the truck. The noise deafened me. Our men shot at the car. One of our trucks chased it down the road.

I laid trembling under Paul's body. I searched the air for a dust cloud. There wasn't one. *Thank God*, I said to myself. At least there's no radiation.

I looked at Jeff. "What the hell was that?"

"A warning. They want us to know they're here. They could have killed all of us if they'd wanted to." He turned to Paul. "Don't you agree, Colonel?"

"Yeah. I do. I'm sure they've watched us for the past couple of hours. Let me check my men." Paul cursed under his breath.

A few minutes later, it was quiet, and all I heard were the sounds of the night. Such was life outside war-torn, destroyed Aleppo. We were going back to the garrison. *Thank God. My head was splitting.*

Chapter 15

Paul jumped up and raced to check the troops. Fortunately, no one was hurt, but the enemy knew we were here. They knew we'd planned to come, and they'd planned to grenade us.

"Who did this? Who threw the grenade?" I asked as Jeff helped me up from the ground. I was sweating, my head pounded, and I felt nausea bubble up into my mouth. I pulled my hair away from my face.

He shrugged his shoulders. "Who knows? It could be just about anyone, perhaps Assad's forces, but my best guess is ISIS. We're pretty sure they're the ones who've been working on chemical warfare in this building."

Several soldiers approached and asked that I return to the truck. I was led away by one of them, and I heard Paul say he wanted to see the grenade so we could possibly figure out who threw it.

I sat in the truck, my head pounding as I watched the platoon of soldiers search the ground around us. It was dark, so the use of searchlights gave it a spooky, eerie feeling. My throat was sore from something. My best guess was the smelling salts Jeff had used near the mass grave. But my judgment wondered if it could've been something I inhaled inside the building. I continued to watch the men search. Finally, a yell went up, and I saw where one of the dogs had found the shell of the hand grenade.

I watched as Paul, Jeff, Sergeant Sneed, and a couple of other men inspected the grenade. I yawned. For some reason, I felt like I needed to go to sleep. I fell asleep in the truck, but I'm not sure for how long. Paul awakened me when he entered the vehicle.

"Sonia, are you all right? You were sleeping." His eyes showed concern as his hazel eyes held my darker ones. "I couldn't stand it if something happened to you." He reached for my hands.

"I... I know. For some reason, I'm so tired I can hardly keep my eyes open." I sat up straight and rubbed my eyes. "What did you find out? What kind of grenade did they use?"

About that time, Jeff jumped in the front seat. His voice was chipper. "I say we blow this Popsicle stand. I've have had all the fun here today that I can."

I smiled. "I agree. Let's get back to post. Was anyone hurt?"

He shook his head. "Nah. We had no casualties. Our men did catch up with the unfriendly who threw the grenade." Paul admitted. "They caught up with him a couple of miles down the road."

I turned toward Paul. "And?" My eyes bored into his face.

"And, what?" He raised his eyebrows and searched my face. His eyes were tender.

"Who ordered it?"

"I'd say ISIS. The dead man was an ISIS fighter. He admitted that before he killed himself." Paul glowered. He looked at me. "Probably sent by your father, but who knows?" A vein popped out in his neck. He was stressed. "No surprise, really. We knew they'd probably been watching this area."

I nodded my head but remained silent. My expression hardened as I thought about my father trying to bomb me to death.

Jeff showed me the grenade he was holding in his hand. "It was a German-made hand grenade. We've gotten Intel that ISIS confiscated twenty-five cases of these from the Kurds a couple of months ago."

"Terrific," I uttered. My voice was sarcastic.

"Let me see it," Paul raised his hand to accept the grenade. "Yeah, it's definitely German. Says so right here." He examined the outer shell of the grenade. "You gotta give it to the Germans. Everything they may make, they make well."

Jeff nodded. "That's true. I wish ISIS didn't have them."

The platoon sergeant opened the truck door. "We got a case of grenades out of the car. These are pretty nice grenades, and we're lucky, and I do mean lucky, that none of us were killed."

"Yeah. That's true. We are fortunate," I agreed. "I just wish it hadn't happened." I know my voice sounded morose and in truth, I was depressed. My head pounded, my eyes stung, and my throat raged with pain.

Jeff turned around in the front seat and gave me a curious look. "Major, this is war. Stuff like this always happens."

I nodded and laid my head against the seat. Paul touched my hand, and for a moment, I felt secure until I remembered that we had almost been annihilated. "Jeff, have you had an opportunity to tell Colonel Grayson and Sergeant Sneed that my father is after me?"

From the look on Paul's face, I knew Jeff hadn't told him my ISIS terrorist father had doubled the anti-for my life.

"What's this, Jeff? Faisal knows Sonia's here?" Paul's voice was harsh and abrupt.

Jeff nodded. "Yeah. He knows. I learned this afternoon. I haven't had a chance to discuss it with you."

I heard the Sergeant groan. Now, he knew I was the child of Emir Faisal Muhammed, second in command of ISIS in Syria and Iraq. I bet that blew his mind!

I offered him an apologetic smile. "Sorry, Sergeant. It's true. Faisal is my father, and somehow, he knows I'm here in Syria. Jeff tells me he's offered up to five million dollars for anyone who delivers me to him alive." My voice was strained and hoarse as I spoke the truth.

Sergeant Sneed gave a short laugh but was poker-faced. "That's all right, Major. We can't choose our parents, or other family members. It's not your fault, and I swear that me and my men are gonna keep you safe." He smiled at me.

"Thank you, Sergeant Sneed." I had confidence in the burly man.

"That we are, Sonia," Paul repeated. "We'll keep you safe. Don't worry."

I thanked the Sergeant and touched Paul's hand with appreciation. The stark truth was that my even being in Syria, at Colonel Grayson's command post, added a considerable level of uncertainty and danger to all the men stationed there. My presence placed the entire garrison in danger. "I think it might be safer for all of us if I work nonstop for the next few days, get a few medical clinics set up, and return to the U.S. I'm convinced that my being here endangers all of you."

Paul turned and gave me a questioning look. "It could be quite the contrary, Sonia. It could smoke your father out to the point where we can apprehend him. Besides, apparently, the Army and the World Health Organization believe you're the best person to turn health care around in Syria."

I listened but didn't reply. There was some truth in what Paul said.

Jeff nodded. I checked his face in the rearview mirror. He didn't look particularly troubled. "Your being here changes nothing, Sonia. Colonel Grayson and his men just happened to be in a hot area right now. In three months, another part of Syria will be overrun with ISIS. I'll check in with my command, but I'm sure they'll want you to continue here for the next couple of weeks." He caught my eyes in the rearview mirror. I nodded.

Paul touched my hand again. "Jeff's right. Your being here possibly ramps up the danger a bit, but not significantly. Besides, we've got the best soldiers anywhere around, and I know Headquarters plans to send me three additional platoons."

I nodded, and my heart rate slowed. I felt relieved hearing this. "When we get to base, I want to start looking through the evidence we collected. I'll need a simple lab with any kind of lab equipment you have, Paul. I can't analyze all of this, but I can do a few things."

Paul nodded. "We'll set you up near the medical area. I've already called ahead and asked a couple of guys to set up some tables and a couple of microscopes." He gave her a sideways look. "Truthfully, we don't have much, but if you get stuff packaged up, we've got a copter leaving at 0600 in the morning. It can drop them off on the way."

My mood brightened. "That's terrific. I'll get all that done after I grab a bite to eat."

"It's spaghetti and meatballs tonight," the sergeant announced, his voice chipper and happy. "At least in the NCO mess tent. Best spaghetti and meatballs you'll ever eat. I can't wait."

I laughed. "That sounds good." Spaghetti and meatballs did sound good to me. My nausea was gone, and I wasn't dizzy. Things were looking better.

Chapter 16

It was after ten in the evening when I entered and looked around my temporary lab. With Sergeant Sneed's help, I pieced together about a dozen test tubes, a glass beaker, and the words poison, deadly, and lethal from scraps of paper we'd picked up. Sneed had identified one of the large pieces of metal as part of a barrel bomb that the enemy had discharged over the house from the air.

"A barrel bomb?" I gasped. Barrel bombs were horrific weapons of terror. A barrel bomb is an improvised unguided bomb sometimes described as a flying IED. Barrel bombs are made from large barrels. They are metal containers filled with shrapnel, oil, chemicals, almost anything, and dropped from a helicopter or airplane. Barrel bombs are deadly due to the large amounts of explosives they carry that can exceed two thousand, two hundred pounds.

"Yeah. A barrel bomb." Sneed gave me a funny look.

I was confused for a couple of minutes. "I didn't know the Syrian Army or Syrian terrorists had used barrel bombs recently – not since Aleppo." I was astonished. Fear traveled up my back.

Sneed motioned for me to walk outside with him where he promptly lit a cigarette. "Yeah, Major. Aleppo was pretty much destroyed by barrel bombs. We still see barrel bombs all the time." Sneed looked at me out of the corner of his eye.

I nodded and moved away from his cigarette smoke. My head still ached badly, and my throat hurt as well, but other than that, I felt pretty good, especially for a girl who'd had a hand grenade thrown at her less than seven hours earlier. I digested the information about the barrel bombs.

"Sergeant, do you have any idea how they killed the civilians at the chemical house? What's your theory?" I stopped and gazed into his face. Sneed was a smart, seasoned soldier. His opinion would be valuable.

Sneed scratched his head, took a long drag on his cigarette, and looked at me. "My best guess is poison gas. Syria has tons of poison gas, lethal stuff, hidden all over. I don't doubt they were cooking up some sort of Kool-Aid in that lab, something they plan to use on another day, probably soon, but I think those civilians were gassed." He turned and looked at me, deliberately blowing his smoke the opposite way. "What about you, Major, what do you think?"

I nodded. Strangely enough, I'd come to the same conclusion as Sergeant Sneed. I smiled at him. "I think you're right. Did you see the bodies of the dead civilians before they were buried?"

Sneed nodded. "Yes, ma'am. And that's why I think they were gassed. It was how they looked, their positions." Sneed scuffed his foot on the ground to get a rock loose that was stuck to his boot. He cleared his throat and turned his head away. I got the impression he didn't want to say anything else.

I was curious. I was also highly complementary of the Sergeant's analytic skills, so I pushed him.

"Positions? What exactly do you mean?" My voice was quiet.

"Well," Sergeant Sneed scratched his chin and looked away from me. His generally lively blue eyes had turned a dull shade of blue. I knew he didn't want to talk about the dead civilians.

His voice was strained and tight when he answered. "I remember how some of the mothers had tried to cover their children's faces with their burkas, probably wanting to keep the gas away from them. Also, there was an older couple holding hands. I didn't see any horrific looks on the victim's faces, and it didn't look to me like anyone had been in pain." He paused, his face sad but thoughtful. "But, it was obvious they'd tried to keep their loved ones away from something." He gave me a sheepish look, "But I don't really know, Major. You're the doctor. You know so much more than me."

I smiled at him. "Sergeant Sneed, I think you're probably, without a doubt, one of the finest soldiers in the United States Army, and your opinion counts one hundred percent."

The Sergeant smiled from ear to ear and bowed his head. I thought I saw a blush creep up his neck. "Thank you, ma'am."

I touched his shoulder. "By any chance, did you take pictures at the site that day? Pictures of the building or the victims?"

Sergeant Sneed shuffled his feet and then stamped out his cigarette. He picked up his cigarette butt and put it in his pocket. "Yes, ma'am. I did. I don't usually share them with anybody, but I take them because it helps me keep my fightin' spirit. The spirit we need to defeat these bastards." He reached into his camo jacket pocket and handed me his phone.

I scrolled through his pictures. Sergeant Sneed was right. The women had all assumed protective positions over their children. The elderly men had tried to protect the women. It couldn't be clearer. There was no question in my mind that my father and his monster mob had murdered these people with some type of poison gas. Anger shot through me as I considered the last few minutes in these innocent Syrian villagers' lives. What had young mothers told their children? What had elderly lovers said to each other? All of this made me sick, angry, and incensed. My father was a colossal brute. To think that I shared his blood made me sick. I was overcome with nausea. I turned away from the Sergeant and felt hot tears burn my eye sockets. I wiped away the few tears that escaped and swallowed the lump in my throat. I turned to face the Sergeant.

I handed him his phone. "I'm sure you're right, Sergeant Sneed. I don't think it was the Kool-Aid, at least not this time. It looks to me like a very quick acting gas. I just wonder how they did it – what I mean is how did they confine the gas to the area where the people were? Why didn't it dissipate into the air?" My insides burned with fury toward the killers my father trained and led to kill innocents.

Sneed answered quickly. "Oh, I'm sure the bastards covered them with four or five canvas tarps. Then, they released the gas remotely. The victims knew there were terrorists standing by with assault rifles that would kill them if they tried to get away. That's how they usually do it. They have a remote detonator. All they have to do is be sure the gas permeates the confined space."

I was outraged when I heard this. It was like teasing someone before you killed them. It was a chicken way to do it. Besides, if I were gonna die and I knew it, I'd want to look at the heavens. *Watch for me Allah, I'm on my way!* But, of course, there was nothing I could do.

I nodded my head as I focused on holding myself together. "You're probably right. I think you'll be my right arm the entire time I'm in Syria," I said with a smile. I'd decided I really liked Sergeant Sneed. He was a good man and a top-notch soldier, but not so hardened in the ways of war that he didn't still feel the pain. I felt proud to work with such a great soldier. Plus, he knew the terrain and had incredible observation skills. I couldn't believe how my soldiering ability had slipped since I'd retired. I'd have denied it if anyone had asked, but in truth, I'd felt it since we'd been back in Syria. What had happened to me? I'd moved away from soldiering, and, worst of all, I'd lost my edge.

Sergeant Sneed grinned at me. I wasn't sure, but I thought I saw a bit of a red flush travel up his face. Had I embarrassed him? "That would be my pleasure, Major Amon. My pleasure indeed. I'd love to assist you while you're in lovely, war-torn Syria."

I smiled and clapped him on the back. "You know, Sergeant, I'm really just Dr. Amon now. I'm retired from the Army."

"Well, ma'am, you're still a major to me! A fine officer." He blushed again, and his broad face turned crimson. His mouth and crinkly blue eyes smiled at me.

I grinned at him as the two of us re-entered my makeshift lab just as Colonel Grayson came in.

Sergeant Sneed saluted him. I smiled at Paul. "Did you get your paperwork done, Colonel?"

He shook his head. "My paperwork is never done, Major. What did you come up with? Any idea what the chemicals are?" He eyed the bundled packages on the side of the room.

"A lot of stuff, Sir," I responded. "I'd like to head to the mess tent and grab some dessert. We can talk there."

"Sounds good to me, Major." He turned to Sergeant Sneed. "Would you like to join us, Sergeant?"

"Thank you, but no, Sir; 0600 comes early around here, and I need to check on my men. Make sure they're all doing well."

"I understand. Good night, Sergeant," I said as the Colonel and I left the tent. "Thank you for all your help."

"You're welcome, ma'am. It was a pleasure working with you. I'll be sure to get all this packed up in the morning and make sure that the evidence gets loaded into the chopper before it takes off."

"Thank you, Sergeant," I flashed him a smile.

"I believe the Sergeant has a crush on you," Colonel Grayson noted as we slowly walked through the compound. "His face is as red as a beet." Paul grinned at me.

"I don't know about that, Paul, but he's a good man and an excellent soldier."

"Agreed, that he is." Paul pulled me over into the shade of a building. "Just don't forget, you belong to me," he whispered in a hoarse voice as he kissed me deeply with the promise of things to come.

I laughed and felt tingly all over. "I won't." I laughed. "Are you jealous of Sergeant Sneed?" Suddenly, my head started to pound again, and I felt dizzy. I decided that after I had my dessert, I was gonna take my own blood and send a sample to the lab for analysis. Something was wrong with me.

"Are you okay, Sonia? You stumbled." Paul stared at me, a concerned look on his face.

"I still have the headache from earlier today, and it makes me dizzy. But, of course, dessert will help." I smiled as I changed the subject.

I took Paul's arm for support and focused on the activities at the compound. Most of the men had gone to bed, but I could see some of them playing cards and talking on their cell phones. Others were on their computers. I reached for Paul's hand. I knew how hard it was to be away from the people you loved. My heart went out to the men so far away from home. I knew how they felt.

Chapter 17

I should never drink coffee late at night, but it tasted wonderful with my cherry pie. I couldn't get to sleep. Even snuggling with Paul didn't help. I tossed and turned in the bed, and re-positioned myself a dozen times. I fluffed my pillow and counted sheep, but nothing worked. I stared at the ceiling for hours.

My mind worked overtime. My body was on high alert from the visit to the chemical site and the grenade attack. I couldn't understand why being attacked had freaked me so much. I'd been attacked dozens of times during my years in the Army, but for some reason this seemed more serious and potentially more dangerous. I lay next to Paul and processed the day in my mind. My conscious mind took me back into the building. In my mind, I walked through the different rooms and looked for clues to help me understand what the terrorists were doing.

And, I remembered the smell. I stared at the ceiling as I gathered my thoughts. I couldn't stop thinking about the bitter smell that had permeated my senses. I believed that smell continued to be the reason I felt unwell. My head threatened to split open, and my eyes burned like torches. I'd been dizzy on and off all evening and even during the night. I'd endured periods where my heart rate soared for no apparent reason. I thought about the smell and decided to ask Sergeant Sneed if any of his men had complained of headaches or dizziness during patrol today when I saw him in the morning.

I lay in the bed, my eyes closed. I tried to meditate but it didn't work. I thought about my mother and how quickly she could go from acute anxiety to utter calmness. Oh, how I envied that.

Suddenly my mind exploded with possibilities. The smell. The smell I remembered was the smell of nuts... of bitter almonds. It was potassium cyanide. I was sure I'd inhaled potassium cyanide. It had to be cyanide. The bitter almond smell was a classic, a legendary sign. I jumped out of the bed, pulled on my fatigues, boots, and Kevlar. I quietly left Paul's room and walked outside into the

cool night where I could think better. I decided to head for my lab. I wanted to draw more blood and send it off for a tox screen. I was curious, though.
How come I was the only one who'd felt bad today? Of course, I'd taken off my
HAZMAT hood and respirator in order to identify the smell. It's likely that's
when it happened. I'd been without my respirator mask, but the cyanide should
have dissipated by now. Lieutenant Handley had been there over a week ago.
Why was there cyanide in there today? How come Lieutenant Handley's people didn't suffer from cyanide poisoning? Or Sergeant Sneed's patrol? *Unless of
course, the terrorists knew we would visit the chemical house today and had deto-
nated cyanide. Could they have been that clever and resourceful?*

At this point in time, these were questions I couldn't answer, but I knew I'd
go back to the house to look again tomorrow, or today since it was technically the next day. I checked my watch. It was a little after two in the morning. I
needed to sleep, but I was in a constant state of wakefulness. Something seemed
off, and I couldn't explain it. It was like I had the sixth sense but couldn't identify the danger. Something was off and wrong. I continued the walk to my lab.
I'd take another blood sample and have it checked for cyanide.

The solitude of the night was comforting. When I reached my lab, I peeked
in on the two injured soldiers. They were sleeping soundly. I waved at the medic
in the back of the room who was playing on his phone.

He stood and saluted. "Major, can I help you?" I shook my head and pointed to the next room and said, "I'll be working over there for a few minutes.
Don't be alarmed if you hear me."

He walked toward me. "Do you need any help? These guys are out like
lights." He nodded at the two soldiers in the beds.

I laughed and shook my head. I noticed he was a handsome man. "Nope. I
just want to go through my samples again and draw some of my blood so I can
send it off for testing tomorrow."

The medic looked at me carefully. "Are you ill? Is there anything I can do
for you?" His eyes were soft, concerned. I liked him.

I shook my head. "Nah. I think I may have inhaled some chemicals this afternoon at that old burned-out building we went through. The one near the
mass grave of civilians ISIS killed a week or so ago."

The medic shook his head and stamped his foot. "The chemical house. That
was horrible. Is there anything I can do for you?" he asked again.

I shook my head. "I don't think so. I'll catch you later," I assured him.

"I'll be here," he said with a smile. "Holler if you need another set of eyes or hands."

"Will do," I promised as I turned and exited the door.

I switched the lights on in my little lab and looked around. Everything was exactly as I'd left it. I wandered over, picked up a tourniquet and needle and the lab tubes I'd need for my blood draw. On a whim, I decided to get a full battery of blood tests. It'd be good to have a baseline, well sort of a baseline, in case anything got worse.

I was actually pretty good at taking my own blood, a skill many hospital people never seemed to be able to actualize. I put the tourniquet on my arm, and quickly drew what I needed. Then I labeled it and packed the tubes in dry ice.

I looked at the broken tubes and bottle we'd collected and hoped for insights that didn't come. After about a half of an hour, I decided I was sleepy and left the lab. I waved at the medic on the way out and walked toward Colonel Greyson's quarters when I heard the unmistakable whistle of incoming RPGs. We were being attacked! The shrill piercing sound was unmistakable, and the entire garrison was awake seconds later.

I immediately stopped and turned my head toward the sound. I could see the RPGs coming toward the compound, like two black dots in the sky. I was startled to note that they weren't just coming toward our compound, but that they had a perfect bead to where I stood. There was a four-foot stone wall behind me, part of a former pre-existing Army camp. A soldier yelled at me to get behind the wall. I was startled at first, but a big guy came and literally dragged me across the ground and put me behind the wall where I'd be safe.

When the first two rockets hit, they landed about a foot from where I'd been standing. I was so shocked that I didn't realize until later how close the hit was. But I knew I had no control and was paralyzed by fear.

All around me, soldiers gathered to return fire. They went through their chain of command, called out orders, and verified them. I remained behind the wall while three other men moved toward a howitzer cannon – their duty station.

The rockets continued to bombard us. There were over twenty in all. The air smelled of smoke and debris. I watched, mesmerized, as the attack continued. I watched a young man, most likely a private, hand mortar rounds to a squad leader who had slapped him in his face earlier to get him out of shock. The squad leader had screamed at him and told him to snap out of it, or we'd all die. My heart hammered in my chest. I could see there was an abundant supply of mortar rails. We couldn't take a hit, and if we did, it would wipe out the compound.

I watched as our men fired. I watch the explosions. I saw the first initial contact and then the secondary explosion as we hit our target and exploded their rounds of ammunition. It was like fireworks I never wanted to see again. All around me, the battle was carried out with perfect precision. Our soldiers responded like clockwork, and their precision defeated every RPG sent at us. The air heated up and the smell increased. It was so hot that the men were sweating.

I continued to watch the fire show, amazed and proud at the team of American soldiers who did their best at what they were trained to do. Each time I heard the unmistakable, shrill whistle of an RPG, I prayed to live, and I prayed for all of those around me to live as well.

After a while, the soldiers first on duty left their post and turned it over to a fresh team. Believe it or not, the first group went to bed, and although it seems hard to believe, they were exhausted and able to sleep during the attack. Perhaps it was pure fatigue, but they did sleep in their Kevlar and helmets between each siren.

I expected the attack to end at daylight, but it didn't. The missiles continued to pelt us. It didn't stop until almost noon. Daylight offered us a clearer target to return fire on.

I stayed behind the wall and watched the brave American men as they returned fire for hours. A couple of times, the men remarked that they didn't know who had attacked us or fired against us. But I knew. It was my father.

Such is the irony of this war.

Around noon, I crawled out from behind the wall and went to headquarters. There, I found Paul and Jeff who were profoundly relieved to see me. I guess they thought I was dead.

"Where were you? We couldn't find you anywhere," Paul scowled. His eyes blazed with fear or anger. I wasn't sure which one. "We were afraid you'd been kidnapped by your father. We couldn't find you anywhere! Jeff and I looked all over."

My mouth fell open as I realized how much I'd terrified him.

For a moment, I couldn't speak, and then I explained where I'd been. I felt ashamed of myself. I believed this attack was about me. *Did my monster father attack an Army garrison simply to take me prisoner? Had he planned for me to face my death as a disobedient daughter of an ISIS leader?* I shook my head as fear gripped my body.

Paul grabbed me and hugged me for an eternity. I looked at Jeff's eyes that were huge as he stared at me from across the table. He shook his head. "I thought we'd lost you. I thought you were gone – either kidnapped or dead."

I shook my head and offered a strained smile. "Nope, I'm alive and well and I promise I'll tell you where I am at all times from now on." I broke my embrace with Paul. "I'm so sorry, Paul. I couldn't sleep and went to the lab to do some work. I didn't tell you because I didn't want to awaken you."

Paul shook his head. "It doesn't matter as long as you're safe. Let's get through this battle and then we'll talk."

"What should I do?" I looked at each of them. For some reason, I felt like a recalcitrant child who needed discipline.

Jeff stood. "Let me take you to your quarters. Paul and I think the worst of this is over. You need to sleep."

Paul kissed me. "Good idea. Keep your Kevlar and helmet on. I'll come to you later when things here have settled down."

I looked at him, tears in my eyes. "I'm so sorry if I frightened you." I was a problem child. I hated myself. I was a pathetic specimen of an army officer.

Jeff walked over, put his arm around my shoulders, and the two of us walked toward my quarters. It was much quieter outside and a lot less scary than during the battle that had occurred at nighttime. I noticed the grim determination on the soldiers' faces. All of them at their battle posts were on high alert.

I walked near the squadron and heard a voice. "Get some rest, Major. We are rocking and rolling today, and we may need you tonight to man a battle station." Sergeant Sneed smiled at me and nodded his head.

I smiled back. "Somehow, Sergeant I think you guys have taken care of it."

Sneed smiled and waved. When we reached my quarters, Jeff walked me inside the small area.

I sat down on the small bed and looked up into his face. His brown eyes looked at me with concern. "Sonia, please stay here and don't leave. Get some sleep. If I can find a spare soldier, I'll stick him at your door. Are your weapons loaded?"

I shook my head. Jeff sat down beside me, and we loaded my weapons. I felt surreal. *What the hell? Did they think Faisal was gonna come and grab me out of my bed?*

Jeff stood. "You okay to be here?"

I nodded. "I'm fine, just fine." I paused. "At least I think I am. Now." I tried to plaster a grin across my face. "Now, get out of here," I joked as I tried to save face.

"I'll be back in a couple of hours to check on you. You're safe here. Get some sleep," he ordered.

I nodded and lay on my bed and, believe it or not, fell into a deep sleep more than likely brought on by fatigue and exhaustion.

Chapter 18

I didn't wake until almost dinnertime. I guess I was exhausted. I was in my own quarters, so I showered, changed clothes, and hiked over for some dinner. I ate alone. I had no idea where Paul or Jeff was. DFAC was essentially deserted, but I was joined by a couple of other officers I didn't know well. I guess they felt sorry for me because I was eating alone. One of them was Lieutenant John Bishop, a close friend of Lieutenant Reid Handley's.

"Major Amon, I heard you saw Reid Handley at Walter Reed. How is he?" The young man's face was sober. I could tell he was concerned about his friend.

I smiled at the young Lieutenant. "Yes, it was my pleasure to see Lieutenant Handley. He was doing okay when I last saw him. As you know, he took in quite a bit of shrapnel, but most of those wounds are healing nicely. I'm more concerned about his radiation levels, but I checked his chart online today and was delighted to see his levels are remarkably low! Believe me, that's great news." I smiled broadly.

Bishop slammed his fist on the table so hard my coffee spilled. "Yes! He high-fived the other officer. That's the best news I've heard for days. So, you think he'll make it?" The guy's eyes held mine. He held himself stiffly as he awaited my answer.

I nodded. "Yeah. I think he will. When initially I saw him, he was weak and in a lot of pain. Once the radiation sickness passes and we're able to build him up nutritionally, get some weight on him, I think he'll be fine. But it's gonna take quite a few months." I reached for my iced tea. It tasted good. I was still a bit groggy from yesterday, and I still had the headache that hammered through my head. Unfortunately, my blood work didn't go out, nor did any of my samples from yesterday. The helicopter didn't come today because of the strike.

Lieutenant Bishop grabbed my hand until I thought he'd shake it off. "Thank you, thank you, Major." His eyes lit up. "Reid and me, well, we've been together since the beginning. He's like my brother. We've taken care of each other ever since college. We were in ROTC together." He paused and smiled as if he remembered something from the past. "We've had a lot of great times. Is it okay if I contact him?"

I nodded and smiled. "Absolutely. If you want to talk to him, give me a time, and I'll have Frances, my administrative assistant, set it up with the nurses at Walter Reed. How's that?"

Bishop was ecstatic. He jumped up, ran around the table, and gave me a kiss on the cheek. "Anytime, I'll talk with him anytime! Just ask her to text me and tell me when. I'll make myself available even if we're in the middle of another strike." Bishop's eyes danced with anticipation at the prospect of talking to his buddy.

My heart soared with Lieutenant Bishop's happiness, particularly after the events of the past twenty-four hours. "I'll email her shortly. Of course, with the time difference, it'll be tricky but Walter Reed, like any hospital, is open twenty-four/seven. I'll get back to you after I contact my administrative assistant. I'll find you and tell you when you can call. Will that work?" I grinned at him.

His eyes glowed with happiness. "Yes, ma'am, yes, ma'am, thank you. If you'd like to text me, that may be easier. I'm gonna grab dessert. Can I get you something?"

I nodded. "Yes, here's my phone number. Send me a text, and I'll have Frances, my administrative assistant, text you directly."

Bishop was ecstatic. "Yes, ma'am. Thank you, ma'am." He paused. "Would you like dessert?"

I shook my head. "Nope, I'm gonna head over to headquarters. I'd like to see Colonel Grayson. Did we have any casualties from the strike yesterday?"

Bishop's smile faded, and sadness flickered across his face. "Yes, ma'am, the terrorists killed two of my men who were out on patrol. Looks like they snuck up on them."

I felt sick to my stomach. I nodded and looked down at my plate. "Sorry for your loss, Lieutenant, for our loss actually. Thank you for the information. I'll keep in touch." I smiled at him. War just totally sucked.

Bishop nodded. "Yes, ma'am, I will. Thank you."

I stood, picked up my dishes, and wandered toward the dessert area. A piece of chocolate cake sounded good to me. I picked up a piece and put it in a box. I turned around and walked out of the dining facility. I stopped by headquarters see if Paul had returned and he had. My heartbeat picked up as I saw him through his open office door in the headquarters administration building.

I cleared my throat, and he looked up. His eyes lit up, and he smiled at me. He stood, came over, and engulfed me in a hug. He kissed me repeatedly. "Sonia. You're awake. How do you feel?"

My dark eyes locked with his hazel ones. "I'm fine, I feel safe now that I'm with you." He gave me a long kiss. Finally, we broke our embrace, and I felt cold again. Paul had always had a way of warming me up. I suppose that's part of love.

"How did we fare during the battle? Was there any information or Intel that they planned to attack us?"

Paul shook his head. "No. Not a shred of evidence or Intel. We had a suspicion something was up but had no idea what or when. There was nothing from our sources, online, or obvious signs of a pending attack on the compound."

I shook my head. "That's just so unusual. There's always something that tips us off."

Paul nodded. "Yep, usually we at least have an inkling. We've had two or three patrols out every single day, and each patrol travels in different directions from the garrison. None of them found or heard anything suspicious – other than the obvious speculation." He shook his head. "It's all very strange. We pretty much always know when the hostiles plan something." I noticed the fine lines around his eyes. He was tired and stressed.

I shook my head. "So, it just happened out of the blue? Has Jeff weighed in? Did he have any idea?"

Paul shook his head. "Nope, not really. Just the usual rumors. That's all anyone knew, at least based on the information we have at this point." He steepled his fingers and searched the reports in front of him.

"What does Jeff say? What does he think?"

"He didn't have specific information earlier. His informants have told him they think ISIS planned something, but there's nothing specific." Paul yawned. "I haven't seen him for the last few hours. I think he left to meet an informant."

I broke away from our embrace and walked a few short steps to his conference table. "Do you mind if I sit? It's kinda weird that Jeff didn't have any information about an attack. He's one of those guys who always seems to know everything."

"Sure. Sit down. I'll sit with you," he volunteered with a smile. "Now, back to Jeff. His people were unaware. They had nada. Jeff has his people searching through Intel they'd picked up over the past couple of weeks, but nothing so far."

I nodded but didn't respond. I was surprised. CIA analysts were the best, and Jeff's team back at the Agency was top-notch. They'd been on point for years. I'd never known them to miss anything in the many years Jeff had been my handler. I took a deep breath and exhaled my anxiety. "Is it possible it was a spur of the moment attack? Perhaps last minute? Unplanned?" I reached for the box with the chocolate cake and placed it on the table. "Oh, I brought you a piece of cake – for being the best CO in the business," I offered with a flirty smile.

"Thanks. My weakness." Paul reached for the cake. I handed him a napkin. "So far, that's all we know. Current Intel reports that Faisal and his nasty band of followers are beefing up manpower. We know there has been an influx of men coming in from Iraq and Turkey to join him. They are definitely rebuilding their forces, and I suspect it's to retake as much land in Syria as the Islamic State had eighteen months ago before we pushed them back."

I picked up a freshly sharpened pencil and drew a couple of lines on the yellow paper. Then I used the eraser to erase the lines. I looked up at Paul. Then I doodled for a bit while I gathered my thoughts.

I knew Paul was staring at me. "What's up, Sonia? What do you think?"

I lifted my face. My eyes bored into his. "I think this is about me. Look at what's happened here - at this compound - just in the few days I've been here."

Paul spread his arms with his palms face up. He shook his head. "Sonia, we have no way to know that. We only have it on rumor that your father knows you're here."

I remained quiet. "Jeff said he knows I'm here." My voice was low, and I heard a quiver of fear in it.

"Is that what you think? You think the compound was attacked because the Emir's daughter is here? You think they attacked us because of you?" His eyebrows shot up, and his voice was a tad sarcastic. It was clear he didn't believe I was the cause.

I looked at him. Our eyes locked. "We've got to consider it. Two men are dead. We've been attacked twice. Once with a hand grenade, and now with a full firefight. There was no provocation for the attack that we know of, so yeah, it might have to do with my presence." My voice was insistent. I was being stubborn.

Paul shook his head. His voice was sharp. "Major, need I remind you that we are at war? That there's a possibility every single day, more than once a day, that our enemy will try to attack and kill us. It's the nature of war. It's why we're here."

I remained silent, my mind and thoughts jumbled. I had to admit to myself that Paul had a point.

"Now, there's no question that your father has more than doubled the ransom for you. He wants to capture you – he has for years. We all know you're an asset – both for your medical skills and your other um, 'talents.' We've used you undercover for years. We've sent you into villages undercover because you look and speak like a local. You're invaluable to us as an asset... and a person. But, Sonia, all of that said, I can't say with any degree of certainty that the attack occurred because of your presence." He paused. "Don't forget, they attacked our patrol at the burned-out chemical house – where we found the mass grave, and there was no plan at that time for you to come here."

I nodded. Paul had made some good points, but the feeling wouldn't leave. I stared at the table and remained silent. I doodled on the legal pad. I wasn't sure what I should say, so I decided to speak from my heart. "I think it's escalated because of me. I can't prove it, and as a matter-of-fact, I have no idea how Faisal even knows that I'm here. How would he find that out?" My face was quizzical.

Paul shrugged his shoulders. "That's a good question. Jeff and I actually talked about that, and neither of us has any idea." He paused for a moment. "In a way, that bothers me from a security aspect. Who stateside knew you were coming?"

I shrugged my shoulders. "I don't really know. Nobody really. It happened suddenly. I'd been in a meeting with a WHO task force focused on improving health care in Syria and the Middle East using humanitarian funds to rebuild parts of the Middle East. When I returned, I had word from Jeff that it was wheels up that evening." I paused. "So, basically I have no idea."

"Jeff told me that he met with his contact, a guy who has been a source for him for years. The guy's a member of one of the rebel groups somewhere in this area. This guy told him that Faisal knew you were here the day you got here."

This shunted fear to my heart. *Who could possibly know I left DC for Syria?* The only person I'd told was my mother. My administrative assistant knew, but she wouldn't tell. She knew how to cover my absences. My voice was shaky. "I don't know Paul, I just don't know. But, we're gonna have to find out."

Paul checked his watch. "It's getting late. I've gotta go. I have a meeting." He took her into his arms. They embraced. "But don't worry, Sonia, you're safe here."

I nodded, but I wasn't sure I believed him. "Okay, I need to go as well. I need to draw more blood and get some stuff packed up for the helicopter. I'm sure nothing went out today." I grinned at him.

Paul grinned. "You're right, that helicopter didn't even get close to here this morning. We sent that message last night at the first sign of the RPGs. Go draw your blood. I'll catch you later - at my quarters." He winked at me, and I smiled.

"I can't wait," I said. I truly couldn't. I needed some human contact. I felt bereft and alone.

A couple of hours later, I walked back toward Paul's quarters. He wasn't in. I fell into bed and asleep still exhausted from the events of my trip. Tomorrow would be a good day. Sergeant Sneed, his men, and I were going to renovate and outfit a building not far away from the mosque as the second medical clinic. The first clinic would be on base. We both felt civilians could easily get to the clinic and would know about us.

I couldn't wait to do something useful. Something good and therapeutic.

Chapter 19

I woke early the next morning, a little after 0600. I was surprised that Paul had already left his quarters. Part of me was disappointed that our love life had suffered this trip. I quickly returned to my quarters, showered, dressed, and pulled my long coppery hair into a high ponytail. I pulled on my boots and headed toward the mess tent for breakfast.

I was amazed at how neat and clean the garrison looked. It was spotless. No one could possibly believe that we were under heavy artillery fire and fighting back as hard as we possibly could twenty-four hours ago. There wasn't a scrap of trash or debris anywhere around the inside of the compound. Heavy plastic containers that had contained sand that had been hit by bullets had been replaced, and any damage in the posts' exterior structure had been repaired. It was amazing. There were absolutely no remnants of the fierce battle that had lasted over ten hours less than twenty-four hours ago. American soldiers were amazing!

I passed the noncom mess tent and ran smack into Sergeant Sneed. He gave me a critical look.

"How you doing, Major? Have you recovered from the battle?"

I gave him a sheepish look. "Good morning, Sergeant. I've recovered. Today's a better day. Don't you agree?"

Sneed gave a short laugh. "Every day is a better day when no one fires RPGs and RPMs and guns aren't blazing. It was an intense battle - especially since we had no idea those bastards were comin' for us." He gritted his teeth as a flicker of displeasure crossed his broad face. It was quick, and then he smiled at me.

I nodded. "Well, I certainly had no idea, but I can say that we held our position well, no thanks to me."

Sneed shook his head. "I heard you took a safe position behind that wall. That was smart – a good place to be," Sergeant Sneed appraised me and smiled. "Nevertheless, you shouldn't be walking around that late at night without an escort." He gave me a fierce look.

"Truthfully, Sergeant one of the PFCs on the Howitzer physically put me behind the wall and told me to keep my head down. It's been a long time since I've been in an active battle. It amazed me that I've medically treated soldiers during active combat and then froze yesterday. Now, they usually stick me in the hospital in the green zone where all I do is patch people up. I don't generally sit through the battle and dodge bullets."

"Well, consider this a battle update," Sneed suggested. "Are you still able to go with me after lunch? My men are working in the old building we decided on for the medical clinic. I thought we could load up some supplies, decide where to put them, and get you to review what we've done. The guys are working now and could use some direction on where to build cabinets and cupboards if you want them."

I was so happy I could have kissed him. *Anything to get out of here and stop feeling useless.* "Absolutely, Sergeant. You've made my day." I smiled and had a hard time not hugging him. "Finally, I'm gonna do what I came to do." I smiled happily at him, and he blushed. If I didn't know better, I'd think the good Sergeant had a little crush on me just as Paul had suggested.

"How 'bout we head out there around one so you can get your lunch first. I'm headed out now, and we've filled a couple of trucks with medicine and supplies. I'll bring half my platoon back and get you and we'll get back out there and get things straight."

I almost squealed with delight. "Thank you, thank you, Sergeant I'll be ready. One o'clock right here."

"Sure thing, Major." He winked at me. "It's a date."

I nodded and waved to him as he walked away. I entered the officer's DFAC and saw Paul, Jeff, and Lieutenant Bishop at a table in the corner. I loaded up my plate with eggs, and biscuits, grabbed juice and coffee and headed over.

"Good morning, gentlemen," I said with a bright smile. "How's everyone today?"

Lieutenant Bishop about knocked the table over when he jumped up to pull out my chair.

"Fine, ma'am. I'm fine today," Bishop said.

Jeff looked at me with a critical eye. "You look rested this morning, Major. What are you doing today?"

I smiled at Jeff and turned to Paul. "Colonel, I must tell you how impressed I am with how things look. The garrison shows no signs of war. No one would know we had a raging battle yesterday." I smiled at him.

Grayson nodded. "Thank you, Major. The enlisted men and officers worked hard. We don't like signs of battle around us."

"Well," I said. "The place looks great."

"Nevertheless, I've requested a couple more platoons. The guys are putting in sleeping quarters down the way. I think they may come at us again," Grayson admitted. "Although, we've no Intel suggesting that."

"The bastards made the decision half an hour before they came," Jeff said angrily. "We know they've stepped up recruitment of fighters and all my contacts - stateside and local - report they want us out of here. ISIS wants control of all the land they held until a few years ago."

Colonel Grayson nodded. "Yeah. That's what we've heard, too. That's why we're getting more men, and there's talk about another command less than twenty or thirty miles away."

Jeff nodded. "That's a good idea. I'll support another Army post. These guys are so committed to jihad, they'll be here fighting when all of us are dead from natural causes. It's for sure the U.S. cannot back out until we've trained a strong Syrian army to take our place."

I felt sick hearing this bleak discussion. I just wanted to get my medical clinics built for our troops and the locals. I certainly didn't want more fighting. I cleared my throat. "Well, sounds like the White House has backed down on troop reduction which is probably good idea."

Grayson nodded. "Yes, thank God! The General said he thought all those conversations had ended."

I looked at Jeff and Paul. "I'm traveling with Sergeant Sneed out near the mosque where he decided to put the civilian medical clinic. He and his men are working on it today. It's near the old market. I'm gonna load up supplies and leave this afternoon, right after lunch."

Jeff objected. "Can you wait and go later, Sonia? I've got a few contacts to see, and then I can go with you."

My eyes caught Paul's eyes and I shook my head. "No, I'm going earlier, after lunch. I'll travel with Sergeant Sneed and half of his platoon. I've been here for three days, and it's finally about time I do what I was ordered here to do." My voice was strong, and I was resolute in my decision.

I saw a quick glance between Paul and Jeff. Then Paul spoke. "I think you'll be safe enough, Major. Perhaps Jeff can join you there after he meets with his contacts. "What do you think, Jeff?" he asked. He looked over at Jeff who munched on a piece of toast. He didn't look happy.

I intervened and spoke. "I'll be fine, Jeff. I trust the Sergeant and his men. Meet us over there when you're finished with your work. Where are you headed?"

"I'll be in and around Aleppo." Jeff's voice was short, his face grim. I could tell he was pissed. Nevertheless, I decided to hold my line. "I'll be happy to see you when you get there." I offered him a half smile.

Jeff nodded, gulped down his coffee, and got up. "Duty calls. I gotta get out of here." He turned his back to leave and then turned back around and looked at me. "Stay right with Sergeant Sneed's men. Don't wander off and don't be in any place alone. We know how badly Faisal wants you. My job," he looked around the table, "is to make sure he doesn't get you." He glared at me, obviously angry that I was leaving without him.

I smiled into Jeff's unsmiling eyes. "No one will get me, Jeff. Scouts honor." I smiled as I wiggled my fingers up in to the scout's pledge. Jeff rolled his eyes and cracked a grin.

"I'm telling you, Sonia. This is a *bad* idea. If Faisal gets you, I may just leave you there," he barked as he left the tent.

I looked over at Paul and Lieutenant Bishop. "He's not a happy camper, is he?"

Bishop remained quiet and reached for his coffee. Paul locked his hazel eyes with my dark ones. I realized he was angry too. "Jeff takes the responsibility of your protection very seriously. You know, Sonia, if Faisal gets you, it's gonna be very hard, if not impossible, to get you back."

A shiver of fear shot through my heart. I knew my father would kill me and take great delight in the process. But I couldn't let that interfere in my work as an Army doctor and now Army War College professor, not to mention my commitment and assignment to the Agency. I responded in a low voice.

"I know that, Paul. I've lived with that fear since I was eighteen years old." I knew my voice was grumpy, but I didn't care. "I won't allow myself to be paralyzed by it any longer." I gave him a long, cool stare.

A flush of anger flickered across Paul's face. I'd made him angry. I was batting a thousand with the men in my life.

I hadn't meant for my words to sting, but they obviously did. Paul clamped his teeth together and shut his mouth. He reached for his tray and nodded at Lieutenant Bishop. "We've got four patrols out, Bishop. Find out which one is closest to the mosque and planned medical clinic and ask them to stay close."

Lieutenant Bishop nodded. "Done, Sir."

Paul looked at me and said, "Stay safe. I'll see you this evening for dinner." He stood, and without another word, left the DFAC.

His departure left me chilled. Usually, we left together. I guessed he was more angry than busy. I rationalized my decision and assured myself that Paul knew I had to do what the Army requested of me - which was to build the medical clinics and investigate for biological agents. That was next on my agenda. I should have the results back tomorrow from the samples that went out early today.

I looked over at Lieutenant Bishop. "Have you arranged a time to talk with Reid? I sent a text last night."

The young lieutenant's face beamed. "Tonight, we're talking tonight. It'll be late for me, but I'll be up. Thank you again, Major."

I nodded and smiled.

Lieutenant Bishop stood. "Can I escort you somewhere, Major?"

I shook my head. "No, you go ahead. I'm going to have another cup of coffee and head over and look through the evidence we picked up at the burn site a couple of days ago.

Lieutenant Bishop rose from the table. "Have a great day, Major."

"Same to you, Lieutenant." I watched him leave the mess tent. Another nice young man.

Chapter 20

I left DFAC alone. I was still smarting from the fact that Paul had left me by myself in the mess hall. Several soldiers set on the deck outside the dining hall. They were playing cards. I smiled and waved at them. I checked my watch and noticed I had about an hour before I was to meet Sargeant Sneed. I decided to return to my lab and focus on finding what had killed the civilians at the burned-out house.

For a moment I was overcome with grief as I remembered the shallow grave. My eyes burned with unshed tears. In my mind's eye, I could see the bodies of the dead Syrian people. I remembered the protective positions the adults had assumed over the children. I'm sure they hoped to the very end that somehow or someway, they'd be rescued. After all, we'd always been taught there was hope. Hadn't we? I could remember feeling fearful and hopeless most of my life. I tossed those thoughts from my mind as I reached my lab. I had to focus on getting some work done. I wanted to get home, back to the United States... at least I thought I did? I struggled with that thought. I was ambivalent. I wanted to be both places. Perhaps my mother was right. My home was Syria, too, and I wanted to help my fellow countrymen escape the chaos and evil that my very own father had caused. I wanted to heal them. I wanted to heal my country.

But I knew I couldn't. It would take a life time for Syria to recover from the recent horrors the country and its people had endured. I sighed deeply as I moved towards my desk. I took a seat and inhaled several deep breaths. My heart beat erratically in my chest and for a moment, my lunch shifted in my stomach, as though it might not stay there. I closed my eyes and leaned back in my chair.

My brain wouldn't shut off. I remembered the shallow grave. I remembered the bodies. My emotions were labile. I went from being tearful to wanting to kill my father and his ISIS followers. I knew he was responsible for those civilian deaths. And a piece of me thought he did it just to show me how despicable and hideous he was. I sat quietly for a few minutes with my eyes closed as I tried to gain control over my emotions.

It was quiet in my little lab. After a few minutes passed, I pulled myself together and got to work. I walked over to re-examine the samples of evidence we'd collected the day before. When I opened the plastic bag that contained a large piece of the tarp that covered the bodies, my eyes stung, and water ran down my cheeks.

I was devastated. My heart beat wildly in my chest, and I could hardly catch my breath.

I knew what had killed them. It was chlorine. The tarp smelled of chlorine. ISIS had used chlorine gas.

My father, Emir Faisal Muhammed had murdered those civilians with chlorine gas. I knew the US Department of Defense had expressed concern and had accused ISIS of using chlorine gas in the past. However, there'd never been absolute proof or conclusive evidence. Now, we had the proof. I had the proof and I had the evidence. It was right here in my lab. The large section of the tarp that my father had covered the bodies of almost 100 elderly Syrian citizens, women and children was now evidence. It was officially a war crime. The evidence was folded in a plastic bag.

Then I remembered a story I'd been told several years ago. A physician friend of mine, the head of a hospital in Damascus, had told me of a family, friends of his, that had been saturated with water and locked in a closet. ISIS had pumped chlorine gas into closet and killed the entire family. The man, his wife and their three young children. For a few minutes I imagined the agony of these last few minutes as their throats became raw and their lungs deserted them. I rubbed chill bumps off my arms. I hoped their death had been swift.

Finally, my cell phone rang and jerked me out of my dark place. It was Sergeant Sneed. I could hear a smile in his voice, and I felt myself smile in return. *How could this war-hardened man be so cheerful? How did he balance the death, the killing, and the wrong and manage to smile? How did he keep those crinkly, happy smile lines around his eyes?* Perhaps I'd ask him. The Sergeant asked me to meet him over in the convey area of the post and I left shortly thereafter.

Chapter 21

Sergeant Sneed picked me up outside my quarters at one o'clock sharp. I'm sure my eyes were still red-rimmed from crying, but the Sergeant knew better than to ask questions. One of his men drove an armored Jeep and a second soldier rode shotgun. Sneed opened the back door for me, and he slid in next to me. His men rode in front of and behind us for protection.

I was excited to see what the men had accomplished. The medical clinic was about a thirty-minute drive north of our Army compound. As always in Syria, and most of the Middle East for that matter, the road was in terrible shape. It was deeply rutted, with numerous potholes and uneven terrain. Oftentimes, our driver had to deviate off the road because of rubble and rocks from bombed-out buildings. I focused hard not to feel dizzy or nauseous. I still had my headache, and my throat was sore.

As we approached Aleppo, I looked at my childhood home. It made my heart heavy. I could still remember the beautiful Syria of my youth. My mother and I often spoke of the beautiful mosques and architecture in Aleppo. It was gone now, reduced to a pile of stone and rubble. Nothing beautiful remained. At least not where I'd been. Aleppo was destroyed, as was Damascus, during the Syrian Civil War. The destruction broke my heart, and told the story of lost ideals, beliefs, trusts, and values. Aleppo told a story of death and lost dreams.

My heart beat quickly, and my blood pressure skyrocketed when I thought about the millions of Syrians who'd been gassed and slaughtered by President Bashar al-Assad, a ruthless man trained as a medical doctor. I could not fathom a physician who murdered. It was the total antithesis to what we had been taught and educated to do ever since modern medicine began. I remembered the news footage as tons and tons of barrel bombs had rained down on the once beautiful city and an early cradle of civilization. I remembered a story of a barrel bomb that fell through the shaft of a Syrian home and filled the house with chlorine as the bomb broke open. The home had become a makeshift gas chamber, quickly killing a husband, wife, and four children with the poisonous gas.

Tears sprung into my eyes, but I held them back. Syria had suffered the tortures of the damned.

I watched our soldiers as they kept their eyes peeled for trouble during our journey. All of us were dressed in full battle gear with Kevlar. HAZMAT suits were packed in the vehicle, and Sergeant Sneed told me there were many more at the clinic's site. It was scary traveling in such hostile territory that was, according to politicians and the media, a non-hostile area. What a joke! I found the concept of a non-hostile area in Syria intriguing. What exactly did that mean? One day, when I had a little more time, I'd think about it.

Sneed touched my arm. "We're almost there, Major. Look ahead." The Sergeant smiled, and his face beamed with pleasure. "It's just up ahead."

I was pleased and surprised when we reached the site of the medical clinic. I have no idea what the original use of the building had been, but now it clearly was a medical clinic. The building was a low, one-story building that had recently been whitewashed by U.S. soldiers. The building was pristine white in the sun, and it made me smile. There was even a blue and white sign that said "Medical Clinic" written in Arabic and English. My head thudded with excitement and pleasure. My eyes teared up and my heart filled with gratitude.

I knew Sergeant Sneed watched me out of the corner of his eye. I smiled. "Wow, this looks terrific! How long have your men been working?"

Sneed's face flushed. "Only since this morning. My men like to do this kind of work. This is much better than dodging RPMs and returning hostile fire." He smiled at me and I returned the smile.

I nodded. "Yeah, no question there."

Sergeant Sneed pointed to a perimeter they had secured around the building. "We'll be putting Tesco steel plates, gravel and sand around here," he exclaimed. "We want people to feel secure, and not scared to come here. If they think it's dangerous or that Assad or ISIS is around, they won't come."

I nodded. "I can't blame them. They'd most likely be terrified," I glowered.

Sneed looked at me. "Well, Major, what do you think?"

"Can I go inside?" I asked as I hopped out of the Jeep. I was truly excited about what these men had done in five or six short hours.

The Sergeant jumped out of the vehicle and came over. "Absolutely, Major. We've done as much as we can without some direction from you. Come in." He walked with me toward the building.

"It's beautiful!" I felt like a child at Christmas as I took the tour proudly accompanied by Sergeant Sneed and his men. "You guys are unbelievable," I gushed as I eyeballed their work.

The building had been separated into four major areas. I quickly identified a waiting room, a small office, three examination rooms, and a larger room in the back where a patient could stay until they were stabilized. A building next to the clinic was a storage area and contained stores of supplies. All in all, it was a fabulous design, more than I would have ever hoped to achieve during the short stay in Syria.

"Well, what do you think?" Sergeant Sneed looked at me expectantly.

I turned to him and threw my arms around his neck. "I think all of you guys are absolutely awesome. Just awesome!" I studied the face of each man and saw appreciation and gratitude from my response. I had made them proud! I ran over, gave each soldier a hug, and told him again how grateful I was for them, for the work they did, and for helping me on the medical clinic. I daresay several of them were humbled, but no one was more humbled than me. Sergeant Sneed had gone thousands of degrees further than I expected.

Sergeant Sneed's face was red as a beet. I'd obviously embarrassed him. He looked at his men and barked an order. "All right then, back to work, the break is over." He nodded toward a couple of soldiers and motioned for them to unload the medical supplies from the truck. He looked over at me. "Major, come with me and tell me where you'd like us to frame in a supply closet or two and also put some cabinets."

"Yes, Sir. I'm coming," I said, my heart jubilant for the first time in three or four days.

I noticed a young man framing in a closet. "We're lucky on this patrol," Sergeant Sneed explained. "We got a little bit of everything. Let me introduce you to Corporal Evans. He's a carpenter and can build just about anything quick as a blink of the eye."

Corporal Evans was young, very young - probably not much over twenty-one.

I nodded and gave him an appreciative smile. "Where did you learn to build like this, Corporal?"

Evans gave me a shy smile. I doubt he'd ever spoken to a Major in the United States Army. His teeth were perfect. "Oh, my dad. My dad builds custom homes back in Arkansas. So, I've been working with him since I was about twelve. I'm a pretty good plumber, electrician, carpenter. Well, I guess I can do a little bit of everything, even some fine finish work."

I nodded. That was impressive. "Well, I can assure you, Corporal Evans, that the United States Army thanks you for your great work here. Can we return to the first room and you suggest were another closet should be? You're probably better at this than I am," I gushed and flashed him my best smile.

"Yes, ma'am." We went into each examination room. "I suggest you turn this entire wall into storage. That way, you can put your patient stretcher or bed over here and you'll have plenty of storage for examination materials and supplies."

I nodded. "That sounds like a good plan. Can you do it?"

Evans squared his shoulders. "I can do pretty much anything you ask for."

I conceptualized his suggestion in my mind and decided it was a pretty good idea. "That sounds great. However, in the room in the back, the room where someone may stay over, I'd call it our acute care room, can you put in a place for a refrigerator?" I paused for a moment and watched Corporal Evan's eyes. He looked confused.

"A refrigerator? You want to put a refrigerator in that patient care area?"

I rethought my request. "Well, we'll need some type of a utility room that has a refrigerator, probably a microwave in case anyone gets hungry, storage areas for intravenous fluids and dressings, as well as some laboratory equipment to run simple lab tests."

Evans drummed his fingers against the sidewall. "Major, is it possible to turn one of the examination rooms into a utility room? Because, if you don't, we'll have to add on to the building," he said as he looked at Sergeant Sneed.

I considered that request. It was unlikely that we'd have three providers here at one time and we desperately needed a makeshift space for a kitchen, refrigeration, and lab. "Sure, I think we can do that." I looked over at Sergeant Sneed. "I think I could set up vaccination clinics outside, perhaps in a pop-up tent."

Sneed nodded. "We could do that. They'd be safe and within the perimeter."

"I think it's a good idea to turn the third examination room into a dirty utility room for lack of another word." I paused and added, "A dirty utility room and a lab."

Sergeant Sneed nodded. "Carry-on, Corporal. You heard the Major," he said with a grin.

"Thank you, Corporal. What can I do? I can paint, nail, or hold boards. I can do most anything," I volunteered. "Please, give me a job."

"I thought we'd move supplies and stock the shelves in the two closets that are built. Is that okay with you?" Sergeant Sneed looked at me.

"Sure, we can do that, but I'd like to whitewash the inside of some of these rooms, just to freshen them up a little bit," I suggested.

Sneed nodded. "We can also do that. And, we have a painter here in our platoon, and he just happens to have a paint sprayer on the truck. Plus, we have thirty gallons of whitewash."

My heart raced with excitement. Sergeant Sneed and his platoon were a gift from God. My eyes sparkled, and I was happy. I laughed aloud and said, "Let's do it."

Several hours later, the men had built shelves in both examination rooms as well as in the kitchen in the acute care area. I could hardly believe it as I walked through the old building.

"What do you think?" Sergeant Sneed asked.

"You and your men are amazing! I never thought we could do this in a day."

I noted a lot of smiles from the men and decided then and there that I would do something special for them. I had no idea what it would be, but they had accomplished in less than twenty-four hours, what I had hoped to accomplish in a week.

"I think that I can start seeing patients in a couple of days. What do you all think?"

I was humbled when a rousing cheer arose among the men. "Yes, ma'am, I think you can too."

Corporal Evans spoke. "What we'll do now is finish emptying the trucks and stocking the shelves. Tomorrow, we can spend the day taking care of any odds and ends that need attending to. He turned to his commanding officer. "Is that all right, Sergeant?"

"It's fine with me if it meets the Major's needs and has her approval."

"Yes, yes. Let's do it!" I looked up at the sky. We were about out of daylight. I looked over at Sneed. "Did you think we should get back to the compound? It's getting dark."

Sneed shrugged his shoulders. "We can, but we have lights, and I think we can illuminate the area well enough so we can get all the supplies in and unpacked if that suits you."

"Well," I hesitated. Something told me to get back to the compound, but Sergeant Sneed seemed so self-assured I agreed.

"What about dinner for the men? Shouldn't we get them back for dinner?" My voice was concerned. I didn't want to push these good men too terribly hard. Besides, who knew, we could have another attack tonight.

Sergeant Sneed laughed. "Major, we have plenty of MREs. The guys will be fine. And they can eat something else if they want to when we return in a couple of hours."

I nodded my head slowly. Although I still felt it best that we return, I let Sergeant Sneed make the final decision. "Okay, Sergeant. Let's carry on then."

Sneed barked orders to his men, and I went over to the supply truck and pulled out a couple of cases of medical supplies. When I looked up, I thought I saw a flash of light a short distance ahead. I continued to gaze in that direction, but nothing appeared. I shook my head and tried to shake off the severe case of the willies that I had.

Several hours later, I practically had a turnkey medical clinic. Sergeant Sneed's men had put together the equipment, the examining tables, and a few chairs. All that remained to be set up was the lab. I walked out to the final supply truck, jumped up in the bed and reached over for a carton of lab supplies. A second later, I was helpless. Someone had grabbed me around the throat. My last conscious moment was watching a firebomb storm into the middle of my newly built medical clinic.

I heard the word "bomb" and saw Sergeant Sneed's men reach for their rifles and disperse. I screamed, "Get out, get out. It's probably radiation."

A minute later, I was unconscious. The last thing I felt was rough hands dragging me over the deserted rubble of the road.

I learned later that the bomb had been a diversion so they could capture and take me to my father.

Chapter 22

Colonel Paul Grayson's face was purple with anger. "What the hell do you mean? Are you telling me that Major Amon is gone? How in the hell can she be gone? There was a platoon of men surrounding her." Paul slammed his fist on the table as his mouth snapped shut.

Jeff put his hand on the Colonel's shoulder, "Paul, this isn't..."

Paul roughly pushed Jeff's hand away. "This should have never happened." Grayson's eyes stabbed Sergeant Sneed's face. He was so angry that he could kill his enlisted man with his bare hands.

Sneed stood his ground as Colonel Paul Grayson shamed and berated him in the Officer's tent.

Paul walked toward the Sergeant and snarled, "What in the hell happened? Where is she?"

"Sir, Colonel, they came in after dark. I don't know how many men there were. They had dirty bombs. We think there were four men, maybe five. "Two of them threw bombs into the medical clinic, dirty bombs." He paused.

"Go on," Jeff encouraged him in a soft voice.

"I heard the Major scream, '*Radiation, Get Out, IED.*' We grabbed our weapons and centered them on the enemy. But there was no one." The Sergeant looked at the floor. "They were gone."

"What the hell do you mean? *There was no one.* You'd been attacked, Sergeant. Where was the enemy?" The Colonel's voice was incredulous. He scowled at Sergeant Sneed. His face was white with anger.

"It was a snatch and run, a grab and get, Colonel," Jeff reminded him. "That's how ISIS kidnaps. They do it every day. They plan a diversion and snatch the victims."

Paul ignored Jeff. He stared at Sergeant Sneed.

Sneed nodded. "That is true, Sir. They did."

Colonel Grayson crossed the distance of his office until he stood inches away from Sergeant Sneed. His speech was compressed. He was livid. His anger and wrath heated the room. "Why did you leave her alone and let her wander around by herself? Why didn't you follow orders and do your duty?" Grayson's face was red with rage.

Jeff, who'd been quiet throughout the interchange stood, "Colonel Grayson, we both know that keeping Sonia Amon from doing what she was determined to do placed the Sergeant in an untenable position."

Sergeant Sneed's face remained unreadable. He looked straight ahead.

Grayson shot Jeff an evil look. "I'm in charge here."

Jeff ignored him. "Nevertheless, we both know Sonia would do whatever she wanted to do, without regard for her own safety. We cannot hold him accountable. Major Amon is complicit in her capture. We've got to admit that and then we've got to get to work and find her because I can assure you, her life window has been cut very short."

Colonel Grayson walked around his office and sat at his desk. "I agree with part of that, Jeff, but my orders were explicit. They were 'don't leave the Major alone,' so, in my interpretation, Sergeant Sneed didn't follow orders."

Jeff nodded. He was weary. "Let's figure out how to move on. "Sergeant, which way did they go?"

"As I said, as best we can tell, several men did a snatch and grab. They dragged the Major down the road to the vehicle they must've had stashed somewhere out of sight. We followed the drag marks of her body to that area. The vehicle tracks suggested they were headed north, or at least we believe it was headed north. Because of the attack and the dirty bomb, and our struggle to return fire, we can't be certain."

Colonel Grayson slammed his fist on his desk "Do you mean you have no idea which direction they took her? This is unacceptable."

Jeff shot Paul a look that begged him to be quiet. "He said the vehicle headed north, Paul, and, your anger isn't helping. The blame game is doing nothing to help us search for Sonia." Jeff glared at him. He wished Paul would just shut up.

Paul glared at Jeff but remained quiet as he paced his office.

Jeff looked at the Sergeant. "That's all right now, Sergeant Sneed. We will take it from here. I trust you'll be around if more Intel comes in?"

The Sergeant's face was impassive, but he nodded. "I'd like to be part of the search, Colonel, Mr. Hansen."

Colonel Grayson shook his head and barked. "Negative, Sergeant." He flashed Sneed a dirty look. "You've done enough damage for one day."

Jeff caught the Sergeant's eye and nodded to him. "I'm sure we'll call on you shortly, Sergeant. You and your men grab some rest while you can. Dismissed."

Paul opened his mouth to object.

Jeff shook his head. "Paul, this isn't his fault. These guys worked like dogs because they wanted to get Sonia's clinic up in record time. Neither of us could've controlled her any better than Sergeant Sneed did. They threw a dirty bomb as a distractor. We can talk about this later. If we are going to find her, we need to organize search teams immediately. Let's send one team in each direction. I need to talk to the Agency and get help. I'll get JSOC in on this. I think they'll help us."

Paul nodded but didn't speak. He looked as though he was off in another world.

"Are you in sync with this approach?" Jeff's voice was loud. "Get some men out there looking while I talk with JSOC and get help."

Paul nodded. "How much time do you think she has before he kills her?"

Jeff shrugged his shoulders. "I'm not sure. It would depend mostly on why he wants her. She has no useful information or Intel. She's not even active Army."

"The bastard wants her because she got away from him all those years ago. Faisal's not a forgiving man. We both know he'll kill her." Paul's handsome face was white with anger. "He'll never let her stay alive."

Jeff nodded. "Yeah. He will kill her, but I think she has a few days. I imagine he wants to settle the score between both her and her mother and that's another story."

Colonel Grayson nodded but remained silent. His hands gripped the sides of his desk. His nail beds were white. He shook his head. He was powerless and hated the feeling.

"My guess is he just wants her because he wants her. He more than doubled the ransom on her head; somehow he knew she was in Syria this week."

Colonel Grayson's mouth flopped open. "Yeah, I heard Faisal knew she was here. How did he know?" His voice was angry.

"I don't know." Jeff gazed at Paul carefully, taking in each of his facial expressions.

The Colonel's nose rattled. "I have no idea. Do you think someone tipped him off?"

Jeff's eyes widened. "Hell, yes. Of course, I think someone tipped him off! How else would he know? We didn't know we were coming until a few hours before we left."

Paul drummed his fingers on his desk. "I found out about the same time you did. You contacted me and told me you'd be in late in the evening."

Jeff shook his head. "I don't know man, but it seems to me like we've got a leak somewhere. Maybe it's on my end – I've been handling Sonia for years. We've never been anywhere before where her father found out where she was."

The Colonel's eyes narrowed. "Do you suggest, or are you suggesting, the breach is on our side?" His face was flushed with anger. "Hell, man. I love her, and I don't know any of my men who would sell her out."

Jeff nodded. "I had a contact tell me the day we got here that Faisal knew Sonia was here. That's how I learned he'd increased the price on her head." He stopped to think. "Anyway, we need Intel on where he's taken her. Can you check with headquarters to see if anyone knows where his camp is? I'm sure we don't have a lot of time."

Paul nodded. "Yes, Of course, I will. We've got to get her back as soon as possible." He sat at his desk. "Let me get some men in here. We'll also track down and kill every ISIS fighter that gets in our way."

Jeff nodded. "You're right about that. I can assure you that Sonia won't tell him what he wants to know, and she won't cooperate with him. He'll probably behead her on television for all the infidels to see."

Paul flopped back in his chair. He was weary and had no clue what he should do. This was much too personal for him to have a clear head. "Okay, man, I'll start at the top, and drop down the food chain.

Jeff nodded. "Good. Also, see if you can get more search groups out, a total of five, work over the villagers, promising anything they want. Give them money. It's in my budget. We gotta get information on where Faisal has Sonia. In the meantime, I'm gonna go work my sources and talk to Washington."

Colonel Grayson nodded. "Sounds like a good plan. I'll inform my men that anything, even the most minute detail, can make a difference." His face was sad but determined. It was clear that Paul was distraught about Sonia.

Jeff nodded and rose from the table. "I'm off. I'll check in with you in a couple hours. In the meantime, contact me if anything pops."

Colonel Grayson nodded. "Will do." His face had a pained look on it. "Jeff, we gotta get her back."

Jeff nodded, walked around, and gave the Colonel a hug. "Yeah, man. I know. I love her too. She's been my responsibility for the past eighteen years."

Chapter 23

I struggled against the two men who had grabbed me in the truck. They were both strong and solid. I stopped struggling for a moment and tried to scream, but a foul-smelling rag was stuffed in my mouth. The only noise that came out was a pitiful cry that embarrassed me, so I gave up.

A couple of minutes later, the two terrorists threw me into the back of an old pickup truck. I laid in the truck bed and looked up at two men, who each had an AK-47 assault rifle pointed at me. After a couple of seconds, I kicked at their legs, momentarily making one of them lose his balance.

I spit the rag out and then screamed at the top of my lungs but was quickly quieted by a hard slap to my face. It hurt like hell and tears jumped into my eyes. One of the guards stuck his rifle in between my breasts. I looked up into his beady dark eyes and saw nothing but hatred and loathing for me and what I stood for. A second later, the other man stuck the rag back down my throat and threatened me with death.

The truck started and raced across the uneven terrain dodging rocks, boulders, and debris. The truck didn't stay on the road. Instead, it traveled off-road at breakneck speed, barely missing old buildings in the dark night.

I laid still in the back of the truck. I was helpless. There was nothing I could do to escape. My father had found me. He was victorious. I knew he'd kill me in a matter of a few hours. I wondered how my mother was and wished I could speak to her again. She'd been so opposed to this trip. After all, Melody had warned me against returning to Syria or anywhere near the lethal clutches of my ISIS father. For a couple of moments, tears streamed down my cheeks as my desperate situation filtered through my mind. I knew my chances of rescue were limited. This was Faisal's stronghold. His most loyal followers were here near Aleppo. No one knew this area as well as my father and his men. Faisal had been born here, lived here his entire life and attended the local mosque. I was sure the men he trusted the most were my guards. They'd also be his most trusted fighters.

Minutes passed as my body bounced up-and-down in the truck moving quickly over the rough Syrian terrain. I imagined the black and blue bruises that would form and swell on my back, shoulders, and hips from the trip. *But they would be nothing next to the beating I'd suffer at the hands of my father.* A few minutes later, I remembered that I wouldn't live long enough for the bruises to turn colors. Once again, hot tears burned behind my eyes. I tried to control their flow, but I didn't do well enough. One of the men with an AK-47 pointed it at my head. He laughed at me when he saw tears on my face. He punched his buddy, and they laughed together at my tear-stained face.

I didn't know how fast we traveled or how long my journey was due to the foul-smelling rag they'd placed over my nose and mouth. I'm not sure if I passed out on my own or whether the substance on the rag deadened my senses. I think it was chloroform. I was in and out of consciousness, so it was impossible for me to determine or judge distance. I tried to listen to road sounds, but I just wasn't alert enough. Whenever I became too alert, the man would put the rag over my nose and mouth again, and I'd be forced to breathe the vapors.

At some point during the night, four men tossed me into a dark room. I remember the men staring down at me and laughing. Maybe it was my imagination, but one of those men seemed familiar to me and seemed to mock me less. I laid on the concrete floor in the room. I was afraid to move around, afraid of what might be there that I couldn't see. I wondered what they'd drugged me with. It seemed like I had constant visions and flashbacks throughout the long, dark endless night. For a moment, I thought I saw my childhood dolls.

I must be hallucinating.

Chapter 24

C IA handler, Jeff Hansen, paced up and down the dirt road in the shadows of an old village mosque. He'd contacted Faiz again, and he had promised to find information about where Sonia's father's base of operations was located. Jeff knew that every hour Sonia was missing would make it harder and harder to find her.

Jeff heard a low voice. He turned, his weapon drawn. Faiz stepped out of the shadows, another man by his side. He embraced Jeff silently and introduced Abdul to him.

Jeff nodded and shook hands with Abdul.

"When did Faisal get her? I knew it would only be a matter of time," Faiz shook his head sadly.

Jeff's stomach churned. "Last night. She was working at the new medical clinic north of the Army compound. Unfortunately, Sonia, being the woman that she is, walked over to unload medical supplies from one of the trucks. She was alone. That's how they got her," Jeff said as he cursed under his breath.

"How come they left her unguarded?" Faiz's face was angry. "They had to know how much danger she was in." His voice was short. "Faisal has wanted his daughter back for years, simply to teach her a lesson." He lit a cigarette and stared at Jeff as though he was a moron.

Jeff shook his head. It was hard to describe Major Sonia Amon to anyone. "The woman is stubborn, deliberate, and tenacious. If there had been ten American soldiers that surrounded her, she still would've gone and unloaded the truck." Jeff paused. "She's stubborn like that."

Abdul laughed. "That figures. I haven't seen Sonia for many, many years, but I can imagine that's exactly how she is today. She was always determined and obstinate." He grinned as he remembered the stubborn little girl from his childhood.

Jeff's eyebrows shot up with surprise as Faiz hastened to explain. He put his hand on Jeff's shoulder.

"My friend, Abdul, and Sonia were childhood friends. They played together as children. His father is a close colleague of Faisal's." He gave Abdul a quick look. "Abdul's father is second-in-command after Faisal."

Jeff's eyes jumped to Abdul's face. His heart rate accelerated. "Dude, you knew Sonia as a kid?"

Abdul nodded. "Yes, I did. As a matter-of-fact, we were best friends and played together almost every day. She used to beat me up when we played hide and seek." He smiled with his eyes as he remembered. "I knew Sonia would leave one day. We talked about it. She had much anger toward her father about her mother."

"So, you've known her for years. Is that correct?" Jeff was shocked. He could hardly believe someone like Abdul existed. In his almost twenty years of protecting Sonia, he'd never come across his name or had any idea the man existed. He checked the guy out carefully. He appeared to be about the same age as Major Amon.

Abdul spread his arms, palms up, as he locked eyes with Jeff. "Yes. I was one of two people who knew Sonia planned to escape the Emir. She spent her childhood telling me how she planned to get away from him. She was determined, and her determination never wavered."

Jeff nodded, and a small smile escaped. "You're correct, Abdul. I would imagine she's not much different." He grinned. "She's as pig-headed as ever!"

Abdul smiled. "I figured she would be. Some spots on a leopard never change."

"Abdul was educated in the United States. He saw Sonia after she escaped Syria. They met once when he was in college. Abdul returned to his country after college and rebelled against his extremist father and the Emir. He joined us in the opposition. Since then, the two of us have fought together against Faisal and President Assad." Faiz smiled at his friend and placed his arm around Abdul's shoulders.

Jeff needed to corroborate the story. He turned to Abdul. "How did Sonia escape when she was eighteen?"

Abdul smiled. His teeth sparkled white in the sunshine. "An elder in the village, a tribal chief actually, who was an enemy of Faisal, gave her a plane ticket. The elder didn't believe in jihad, and he abhorred violence. He'd hated the way the Emir had treated Sonia's mother. In fact, he called a Tribal Council about it which caused him great trouble down the road."

Jeff nodded. "Where's this man now?"

Abdul lowered his eyes. "He is dead. He's been dead for many years. Faisal learned he was complicit in his daughter's escape and had him beaten." Abdul hung his head. "He didn't live long after the beating."

Jeff had to admit to himself that the man's story had truthful elements. He'd known about the old man giving the ticket to Sonia. He didn't know about his death.

Jeff turned to Faiz. "Is this a story you can vouch for?"

Faiz nodded his head, his voice definitive. "Abdul and I have fought side-by-side in battle for many years. I was not in the Emir's camp as a child and a young man. But I can say to you in all truthfulness that this is the story he's told me for almost twenty years, so I have no reason to doubt him."

Jeff nodded and looked at Abdul. "How long do you think it will take before Faisal kills her? How long do we have to find her?"

A look of frustration flickered across Abdul's face. "I would say no more than three days. ISIS and Faisal will spread this all over the Western media. I would anticipate this morning he will have her denying her American values, condemning the United States, and telling lies about the United States Army." He shook his head. "That's part of the ISIS way. Of course, there'll be a masked executioner behind her as she refutes her beliefs."

Faiz nodded. "I agree. Then he'll have a trial, and she'll be condemned and sentenced to death. Most likely, her execution by beheading will occur on the third day - two days from now." He hung his head in shame.

Jeff nodded. "So, there's no reason to expect him to treat his daughter any differently than the rest of the 'infidels' he kills."

A flicker of uncertainty crossed Abdul's face. "Probably not, but she may live a few days longer. But more likely, he will be harsher with her than others." Abdul scratched his beard. "At least, that's what I think."

"It's what I've always heard," Faiz agreed.

Jeff leaned against the wall of the old mosque as he processed Abdul's information. "Will you tell me about your father, Abdul, and his relationship to Faisal?"

"My father is the Emir's closest friend, his closest ally, and his most trusted warrior. They are like brothers and share the same beliefs and ideology. My father is technically one of the leaders in ISIS."

Jeff nodded. He wasn't surprised. "What's his name?"

"Jazeed Abuwari. He is well known." Abdul's face was a mixture of disgust and hatred. "Faisal would trust him with anything. Even the death of Sonia."

Jeff nodded. "Yeah. I know him." He paused, "Anything else I need to know?"

Abdul shook his head. "No, man. We've just gotta find her. He will kill her, and if she makes him angry, he'll kill her sooner."

A wave of fear crashed through Jeff. It was so frightening that he almost fell to his knees. *Would that crazy son of a bitch kill Sonia?* He steadied himself for a moment, caught his breath. "Abdul, do you have any idea where he is? Do you know where he could be holding Sonia?"

Abdul motioned him closer, using his index finger. "Yes, I'm not certain, but I'm almost sure."

Chapter 25

J eff returned to the compound and searched for Colonel Grayson. "I have some information. I think I may know where Faisal has Sonia."

Paul's eyes lit with anticipation. "Where?"

Jeff paused as his satellite phone rang. He held his finger up. "Hold on. I've got to get this."

Jeff turned his back and walked out of the Colonel's office. He spoke in low tones with a colleague at Langley. Paul's anxiety escalated as he watched Jeff's body movements. He knew the news was probably bad. He fortified himself for the worst. Grayson watched as Jeff terminated his sat phone conversation and re-entered headquarters.

Grayson's body posture was stiff and wooden. His eyes searched Jeff's as he waited for him to speak. Jeff sat down at the Colonel's conference table and made a few notes.

"What, what was that all about, Jeff? What'd they tell you at Langley?" Fear was palpable in Paul's low-pitched voice. "What do you know?"

Jeff looked up and gave Paul a tired look. "They have nothing on Sonia, but I think we've found our leak. It looks like they've taken Melody, Sonia's mother."

"Melody?" His voice was incredulous. His face paled. "You think they snatched Melody as well? From the U.S.?"

"I can't say for sure, but I certainly suspect it. Give me half an hour, and I'll tell you. I need to contact the locals and have them check her place and look for her."

Jeff disappeared into his office to make some calls. An hour later, he reappeared. The Colonel was seated at his desk. "What did you find out?" Paul's anxiety marked his face. His face was lined, and his body movements quick as he stood to acknowledge Jeff's presence.

"We've just had a team sweep Melody's townhome. She's gone, and the place has been ransacked. They've found three bugs there. ISIS, or at least we think it's ISIS, planted bugs in the living room, kitchen, and bedroom. That's how they knew Sonia was headed to Syria." Jeff's face was red with anger. "Those bastards are one up on us this time."

Paul shook his head. "How long has Melody been out of witness protection? It's been a good while hasn't it?"

Jeff nodded. "Yeah. A couple of years, I think. I imagine they found her once Sonia retired. The two of them are together often, probably three or four times a week in the beginning and probably just as much now."

"How long has Melody been gone?" Colonel Grayson's face was pale as he put the pieces together.

"From what my team told me, it looks like she was snatched on Saturday. It's been two days. Her neighbors last saw her on Saturday. No one has seen her since."

"So, they took her the day after you all got here." Paul shook his head. "I wonder if she's even alive."

"And, being the weekend, I guess they didn't expect her at work, did they?" Paul was obviously upset. "So, no one missed her." He slammed his fist on the table as he thought about Sonia's sweet, trusting mother. Hadn't she seen enough hell in her life? She'd married what she believed was a good man of Islam who'd radicalized and become a terrorist. He was one of the most feared men in the world. He'd beaten her, stolen her child, and still wasn't finished. "He'll kill her for sure. There's no question in my mind."

Jeff nodded. "That'd be my guess. I gotta hand it to the Emir. He's pretty smart, not to mention he's a vengeful son of a bitch."

Paul sat at the conference table, his face white with anger. "What do you think the chances are that Melody is still alive?"

Jeff contemplated this for a moment. "I think they're both alive now. But, of course, not for long. I'm sure Faisal has something horrific planned for them. He'll most likely make a statement soon and announce a memorable and horrendous death plan."

Paul's fingers gripped his desk. His nail beds were white. He shook his head. "Oh my God. I can't imagine what he'll do. We've got to find them!"

Jeff nodded. "We don't have a lot of time. I'm sure he'll ask for the President and the United Nations to return all captured ISIS terrorists and Al Qaeda fighters. And, of course, they won't." He shook his head and collapsed in the chair.

Paul shook his head. "No, they won't because we don't negotiate with terrorists. Our only hope is that we can find them and find them quickly."

Jeff steepled his fingers. He was deep in thought as he considered the situation. "You're right. I think the White House and JSOC will intervene if we can find where they are. They're working on a plan." Jeff's voice was cautious.

Paul jumped from his desk. "For God's sake, man, what kind of plan?"

"I'm not sure yet. I think I may know where she's being held. I need your best men to go search with me tonight."

"Take anyone you need. Take anything you need." Paul returned to his chair and laid his head on his desk. He was tormented, and in such angst, that Jeff went over, and grabbed his shoulder.

"You gotta get hold of yourself, Colonel. I need you at your very best to help me find Sonia. I've gotta go out. I have some more people to talk to, and I'll be back soon. Keep those search teams out and about. Have them talk to every villager and every friendly they can find until something breaks. We don't have a lot of time. Trust me, somebody knows something!" He paused. "Someone knows something, they always do."

Paul raised his head, nodded, and locked eyes with Jeff. "Will do, Jeff. I'm okay. I just love her, that's all."

Jeff nodded and smiled. "I know. It's a tough situation, Paul. But we haven't lost yet. I love Sonia too."

Paul nodded and cracked a weak smile. "I know you do. You're like a brother to her. Catch up with me later."

"Will do," Jeff assured him as he left the room.

Chapter 26

I couldn't believe it! I looked around my childhood playroom. In truth, my father hadn't changed a thing. It was the same. My dolls were on the same shelf as always. My favorite books were lined up in the same order as I'd left them. My stuffed animals were arranged according to color, as they were when I was ten years old. My eyes continued to view my childhood playroom located in the old barn adjacent to my father's residence. The flood of emotions paralyzed me. Tears stung my eyes. The good memories of my father hammered at my heart. I saw the doll crib he'd made me when I was about two or three. It was my first real memory of him. We'd painted the crib a pale yellow, and my mother had hand-sewn sheets and blankets for the bed. Tears ran down my face as I reached to touch the crib only to realize I couldn't reach it. I saw my basketball and remembered that I'd loved that game because I'd seen it on American television. My father had purchased a basketball for me from America and had it sent here. I used to play hoops behind the old barn where I was now being held captive. I figured I'd probably die in this very room where I'd spent so many days as a child with a man I believed to be good, kind, honest, and true to Islam.

The first hot tears sprung from my eyes. I struggled to hold them back. I wished I had Tessa with me. At least I'd have something I loved to hug. But, Tessa was home, hopefully running the fields and completely happy. Tears ran down my cheeks as I thought of my beloved dog.

The irony of it all.

As I lay on the floor and reminisced about my childhood, I wondered what my father had thought all these years. Did he believe I'd returned to Syria? Did he think he would be able to win me over to jihad? There must be something, some reason why he'd kept my toys, my youth untouched. He must have had hope. Otherwise, why wouldn't he have gotten rid of his memories of me, why wouldn't he have gotten rid of my bedroom, my dolls, my games, and my books? As I lay there, I shivered when I wondered what he planned to do with me.

I'd fallen asleep again on the hard floor when the door opened. I kept my eyes closed and pretended to be sleeping. I had no idea who'd entered. A boot kicked me in my hip. A searing pain traveled up my back. I swear I could feel a ping in every spinal nerve I had. My eyes flew open. I looked up into the dark, unreadable eyes of Faisal Muhammed, the second in command of the terrorist organization, ISIS.

My father.

The two of us stared into each other's eyes, but no words were exchanged for a lengthy time. The silence was exhausting. It fatigued me, frightened me, and shattered my self-esteem. I held my eyes with his until he spoke. I didn't blink or look away. I didn't falter.

"You haven't changed much, Sonia." His voice was raspy, most likely from many tokes on the hookah pipe. It was also gruff, probably from shouting orders to his men. The soft, undemanding voice from my childhood was gone.

I didn't respond.

"You look the same as you looked as a child." He continued to stare at me until little prickles of fear raised up on my arms. His cold eyes traveled the length of my body as dread and terror engulfed me.

But I didn't waver or vacillate. I stared at him and spoke. "I cannot say the same about you, Father. You look much older, very fatigued. War-weary, one might say."

He stared at me but didn't reply. I supposed it was my time to speak, so I continued.

"Have you enjoyed your life of murder and destruction? Did you take pride in the destruction of our hometown, of Aleppo? How many thousands of people are you responsible for killing?"

Faisal raised his bushy eyebrows as I saw a flush move up his neck. He was angry.

I was furious, vehement. I couldn't stop insulting him. I suppose these were things I'd wanted to say to him for years but never had the chance. I'd been terrified of him as a little girl, but I'd tried hard to win his attention. I painted him the best pictures; I colored within the lines to make him proud. As a teen, I'd mostly ignored him, but I remembered how I'd tried to win his approval. Nothing had ever been enough.

But now, I hated him. I loathed him for stealing my mother's life, for shattering my life. My father, my flesh and blood, was responsible for the devastation of a nation, and the murders of countless numbers of men, women, and children. My father murdered without provocation. He gassed and poisoned old men and women, and never gave it a second thought. He murdered children and babies, and it didn't faze him at all. He was a monster.

Faisal gave me a patient look and shook his head as if I was a recalcitrant child. "Those people were our enemies. They are enemies of Islam. This is jihad. This is a holy war. We are following the teachings of the Koran and Sharia Law. I hope you will one day understand."

I looked up from the floor, startled by a noise. I saw three men, Faisal's bodyguards, enter the room. They had AK-47s trained on my head. I shook my head, my voice was defiant. "I will never conform to your way of life. I am a doctor, a physician. I save lives. I don't take them. You're a butcher." I spat on the floor.

My father glared at me and slowly shook his head like I was a disobedient child. His look pitied me, but then turned to a scowl, and finally a snarl. Rage rolled off his body. I could feel the heat. He continued to stare down at me.

I'm sure the look of disgust on my face inflamed him. His pupils dilated, and he nodded at one of his henchmen. "Carry on." Then, my father left the room with a single bodyguard. The other two men re-tied my hands and feet and proceeded to beat me. I felt my right shinbone crack and knew immediately that my leg was broken. My terror mounted as the men covered my face with a black hood and began to strangle me. Each time I thought I was dead, they let me breathe. It was serial strangulation. My chest burned from a lack of oxygen. My head roared in pain. The torture was horrific. It was all I could do not to cry out and scream, but I held my tongue as silent tears shattered my senses.

I don't know how long the beating lasted, but it felt like an eternity. I was barely alert when my father's henchmen left, my mind muddled, my thoughts jumbled up. I looked at the stars on the ceiling in my bedroom. The stars I remember my mother gluing on the ceiling when I was about three years old - just before we escaped to the United States. I fell asleep. I think I whimpered for my mother, or perhaps it was just a dream.

But I was in pain. So much pain. My body and my mind. I knew I'd die from the next beating.

Chapter 27

It was almost pitch black, several hours past midnight, when CIA operative, Jeff Hansen, and Sergeant Sneed crept through the shadows toward the home and compound of Emir Faisal Muhammed. Their military grade night vision goggles were attached to their helmets and eliminated the need to carry flashlights. Their hands were free which allowed them to carry weapons and other gear. Faiz and Abdul approached on the opposite side of the compound.

"How many guards do you see, Sneed?" Jeff crouched on his hands and knees to stay invisible.

"I see four at the main house, and four surrounding the other building, the barn I guess, since cows and goats are penned up there."

Jeff nodded. "Yeah. Copy. I see the same. There's also four more around that long building, the bunkhouse. I suspect that's where his closest followers live."

Sneed cleared his throat and cursed. "What else?"

Jeff squinted to see more clearly in his night vision glasses. "Well, we're looking at twelve terrorists; four surrounding each building, plus the perimeter guards we passed. So, sixteen in total."

Sneed nodded. "Yeah. So, to get to the house, we'll have to take out at least sixteen men before we even get close to the Emir and finding Sonia." He cursed under his breath. "A piece of cake. My men can take these shit head bastards out in a heartbeat." The Sergeant's voice was clear and strong. "Not a problem, Sir."

Jeff nodded. "We're getting additional help, just in case. I've been in contact with JSOC, and as soon as the White House agrees, we'll have Delta Force here."

"I love hearing that." Sneed grinned from ear to ear. "They'll take all of these SOBs out, plus get Sonia and her mother out of here in no time flat! Delta rocks."

Jeff nodded. "That's the plan. What do you think we'll find inside the house? You think there are more guards inside?"

Sneed nodded. "Yeah. Abdul said there are a bunch more guards. The Emir sleeps on the top floor. I suspect the first two floors are nothing but guards. Remember, this is the bastard's stronghold."

Jeff nodded. "Yeah. Sonia told me years ago that her father slept on the top floor and sometimes on the roof, especially when it was hot. I doubt that's changed."

Sneed shook his head. "It's the best place. He's got two floors of men underneath him for protection and is in a strategic place to use firepower. I bet he's up there now. I wish we had heat signatures to validate it."

"We'll validate it before we go in. I've got people coming, so we'll be able to gather some heat signatures before too long. We've arranged for Kurdish aerial surveillance to see what's in the house or at least give us an estimate."

"Where do you suppose he's holding the Major? You think that terrorist son of a bitch has her in the house?"

Jeff shrugged his shoulders. "I don't know. Hopefully, the Kurd's aerial aircraft will give us that surveillance. My best guess is that she's here, but it's possible he could have moved her almost anywhere. We just don't know."

"You think her mother's here?"

Jeff nodded. His night goggles moved back and forth on his head. "Yeah. I do. Knowing Faisal as well as I do, I'd bet he has some disgusting plan to kill them together or pit them against each other. He'll probably kill one of them in front of the other and upload it to YouTube."

Sneed replied with a long list of whispered expletives. "I want to kill that man. I want to kill him bad."

Jeff chuckled. "Yeah, you, me, the Colonel, and half of the free world. You'll have to stand in line, but maybe you'll get your bullet in before all is said and done."

The men continued to watch the compound for about half an hour. No one came or left from the buildings. Sneed lowered his night goggles and checked his watch. "We gotta go, Jeff. We need to figure out what Faiz and Abdul have found."

Jeff nodded, and the two men wandered carefully through the dark night to meet up with Abdul and Faiz. They loitered behind trees near the recon area that they'd set up earlier.

"What'd y'all see? How many terrorist guards?" Jeff's voice was low.

"We counted a total of twelve, four on the house, four on the barn, and four on the bunkhouse." Abdul looked at Faiz for agreement. Plus, we counted four men on perimeter watch. So, sixteen men."

"Yeah, I agree. A total of sixteen men we need to take out fast. But we can do it." Abdul's voice was eager.

"Yeah, At least sixteen, plus whoever's sleeping in the long building." Sneed corrected, "And up in the house where Faisal sleeps."

Abdul nodded. "There are probably twenty or twenty-five more men sleeping in the bunkhouse. We've gotta do something to neutralize them." He looked at Jeff.

Jeff smiled. "Don't worry, Abdul. We'll have more firepower than you can possibly imagine. They'll all be gone in twenty-four hours, and this mission will be history. Sonia and Melody will be back in Washington. In the meantime, let's coordinate aerial surveillance. I want to know where the heat signatures are before I relay any information back to the states." Jeff gave the men a confident smile.

"Yeah. Sounds good. Do we have help with that?" Abdul frowned.

Jeff nodded. "Yeah. The Kurds will help us. They've got a small plane that leaves no heat signature. The exhaust ports are on the top of the plane, and that reduces the infrared signature. It'll keep the plane from showing up on any ground-based heat sensing system. Faisal won't detect us."

"Does he have a ground-based sensor?" Sneed arched his eyebrows. "That's pretty sophisticated."

Abdul nodded his head. "Man, Faisal has everything. You all would be shocked. He's the purse strings of the operation. I am sure he does." Abdul looked at Faiz. "Isn't that what you've heard, my friend?"

"Yeah. I'm sure he has a heat sensor. At least it's been rumored that he has one at his home compound and another at the main ISIS fortress closer to Damascus. It's on the roof of his residence." Faiz's voice was quiet but assured.

"Then we go with the plan that he does," Jeff decided. "We'll still be able to validate with the aerial surveillance."

Abdul nodded. "Yeah, that's the best decision. At least it's been rumored enough for me to believe it." He shook his head. "I don't think it's ever been tested. Frankly, no one has had the balls to attack Faisal at home." He smirked. "I can't wait!"

"The Kurds have been our ally in this war since day one," Jeff remarked. "But, that's terrific, Abdul. Now, let's get out of here before someone sees us and we're turned into toast."

The four men were silent as they walked down the road to the truck that was parked several miles away. Jeff looked at the sky and was thankful the moon was only a sliver of light.

Sneed spoke as the four men got in the truck. "Tomorrow night will be a perfect night for us. It'll be dark as Hades out here. There'll be no moon. I can't wait to get this bastard."

His companions grunted in agreement.

Chapter 28

Jeff entered Colonel Grayson's office, his satellite phone in hand. A look of anxiety stretched across Grayson's face. He sat behind his deck, paralyzed by anxiety.

"Jeff, what do you know? You heard anything about Sonia?" Grayson's voice was low. He tried to smile, but his mouth was twisted.

"Sonia's on television. Get on your computer and go to CNN."

Paul grimaced and turned his computer to CNN breaking news. Sonia was on the screen, bruised, battered, bloodied, and defiant. Behind her were three armed men. One man, obviously the executioner, wore a black hood. He brandished a small knife. Two ISIS terrorists holding Colt M16 assault rifles flanked her. Sonia's face was openly rebellious and stubborn. She turned to the terrorist on the left and said something. He pointed his assault rifle at her head.

"She's not giving in, is she?" Jeff remarked. "I know she realizes we'll come for her. I don't want her to get him so angry he kills her quickly." Jeff's face was troubled as he sent Sonia a telepathic message to be more compliant. She was one stubborn, defiant woman.

A vein throbbed in Paul's neck. His chin jutted out. His anger was palpable. "Look at the size of that knife. It looks too small to behead someone."

Jeff shrugged his shoulders and looked away. "ISIS always uses small knives to behead people. You know that. You've just forgotten. They like to inflict as much pain and prolong the process for as long as they possibly can so the victim will suffer."

Paul paled and clasped his hands over his head. His face contorted. "How long do you think we have to rescue her? I'm sure Sonia will settle down. She'll know how to play this out, particularly with her father." His voice was matter-of-fact. He hoped he was correct, but he wasn't sure.

Jeff nodded, but he wasn't quite as sure if Sonia would play it safe. He was in unchartered waters and wasn't sure what Sonia would do. He knew the depth of hatred and disgust Sonia had for her father. He prayed her fury and rage didn't interfere with her judgment. He hoped Faisal had kept her away from her mother. The chances were very high she'd lose it if she knew Melody had been captured as well.

"Well, we can't control her. She'll say what she says." Jeff's voice was strained. "I figured he'd put her on TV, make her describe the United States as an imperialistic country or some such crap – you know, the same old, same old. Then he'll have some stupid mock trial... so," Jeff looked out the windows, "two days max."

Paul's face contorted with anger. "She'll never support the caliphate or jihad, nor will she denounce her American citizenship. She'll opt for death before she'll convert." Paul assured him. "I'm sure of this. We've discussed it."

Jeff nodded. "Yeah, she's said the same to me. She's stubborn and determined. We can't control her at this point, but we can hope." He stared at Sonia's image on the screen. "She looks pretty okay. Looks like he's beaten her, but she still seems to be with it."

Paul held up his hand. "Quiet. She's speaking."

Jeff stared at the computer screen as his heart pounded in his chest. Sonia lifted her chin and pursed her lips. She looked defiant and angry. Her brown eyes blazed with contempt for everything around her.

"Uh oh. This isn't good. She's gonna blow this!" Jeff's voice was low, fearful. Fear inched up his spine. "She's gonna blow it."

"MY NAME IS DR. SONIA AMON. I AM AN AMERICAN CITIZEN, A DOCTOR, AND A RETIRED ARMY OFFICER. I AM IN SYRIA TO HELP REBUILD THEIR HEALTH SYSTEM WHICH MY FATHER, EMIR FAISAL MUHAMMED, DESTROYED. MY FATHER IS A MONSTER, A MURDERER OF CHILDREN. HE IS..."

The video camera wobbled and the picture cut in and out. Two men grabbed Sonia. She was beaten repeatedly with the assault rifle, but not one sound was heard. Sonia did not cry out.

Paul's mouth flopped open as his eyes widened. Fear clouded his vision. His body hunched forward as he wrapped his arms around himself. "Good heavens, Jeff. He's beating the hell out of her. They'll kill her if he doesn't stop them. They hit her in her face. Look at the bruises." Paul enlarged the image of Sonia's head until it covered his screen.

Jeff grabbed the mouse. "Don't torture yourself, Colonel. We've got a long way to go, but help is coming."

"What help?"

Jeff gave Paul a sly look. "I know where Sonia is, and I have to assume Melody is there as well. He's holding them at his compound, also his home. Last night, with the help of the Kurdish Army, we determined heat signatures of possibly as many as a hundred plus ISIS terrorists surrounding the Emir's compound."

"Is that all? If so, I'm surprised." Paul's face registered disbelief.

Jeff shook his head. "No. The Emir has a large rectangular structure to the left of the main house that most likely serves as a bunkhouse for his terrorist guards. We're not sure how many, as the whole building appeared to be a heat signature. In addition, we found another floor in the main house that appears to be a bunkroom for terrorists. It's located directly below the floor where Faisal sleeps. I imagine they're his most trusted men." Jeff paused. "Plus, his main force is in Damascus, and there's a stronghold near Aleppo."

"What about Faisal?" Paul seemed subdued.

"We assume he's there and he's ordering the torture."

Paul nodded. "Anything about Melody? Any sign of her?"

Jeff shrugged his shoulders. "Not specifically, but some of my Intel did report they'd seen a very white-skinned woman dressed in Syrian female attire placed in a truck and driven out of Aleppo. We can only assume it was Melody." Jeff rubbed his temples. He was tired and needed to grab a few hours rest before the mission.

Paul steepled his fingers as he considered Jeff's Intel. "What else do we have from the sweep by the Kurdish aircraft?"

Jeff thought for a moment. "There were a few heat signatures we picked up in the barn. I don't know if they're farmers or people that care for the livestock, but it's possible that's where they're holding Melody and Sonia."

Paul sat back in his chair and put his legs on his desk. "Should we plan to attack?"

Jeff nodded. "Hell, yes we're gonna attack. Melody is the daughter of a distinguished American diplomat who still has friends in high places. Sonia is a decorated, recently retired, Army Major, and a professor at the Army War College. Her career has been impeccable. Emir Faisal Muhammed is one of the most-wanted men on earth and for years has shattered the lives of Melody and Sonia."

"No argument from me. Is the White House on board?" Jeff and Paul both knew that only the White House could approve an extraction by Delta Force.

Jeff nodded. "I've presented this information to JSOC who has come up with a plan. Pending White House approval, Delta Force will extract them."

Paul's face brightened. "When?"

"Tonight."

"Any anticipated problems from the White House?" Paul was so attentive that he looked as though he was carved in stone.

Jeff shook his head. "Nope, not a one. They're on board. It's just a formality."

Paul jumped from his desk and high-fived Jeff. "Man, this is the first time I've had any hope at all since they took her. There seems to be a chance we'll get her back."

Jeff grinned and there was a fire in his eyes. "What do you mean a chance? We're getting them. Both of them. Tonight."

Chapter 29

I stared at the wall in my room, looked at my collection of Barbie dolls untouched for years on my bookcase as I contemplated my chances of escape. I knew it would be hard, particularly since I'd been beaten. I knew that Jeff and Paul would come for me. I just didn't know when they'd figure out where I was. I was bound tightly and tied to the day bed I'd napped on as a child. I worked hard wiggling out of the bonds. I could feel sticky, warm blood drip down my fingers. Then I slipped out of the rope and untied myself from my bed. I was so exhausted from the task that my beaten, frazzled mind fell asleep.

I woke suddenly. I heard a lot of noise below in the courtyard under my window. I thought I heard someone scream. It sounded like a woman.

I painfully inched myself across the floor. When I couldn't inch any further, I crab-crawled. I climbed up an old rocking chair, the same rocking chair my mother used to rock me to sleep when I was an infant. We'd talked about the chair many times since we'd been reunited. Fortunately, the rocking chair was heavy and stayed in place as I climbed up on it. I managed to place my elbows on the windowsill to brace myself. I put my useless right leg in the seat of the chair to brace it against the pain of gravity. I looked out of the window.

A crowd had gathered in the courtyard below. At first, I didn't understand what I saw. But, after a few minutes, it dawned on me that it was some sort of tribal meeting. For a swift moment, my mind remembered the elderly tribal chief who'd been responsible for my final escape so many years ago. My father had stolen his title. Now, my father sat on the "throne," a large wooden chair, and was obviously in charge. There were men everywhere, and as usual, he had three terrorists standing behind him and one on either side. All five men held their assault rifles in a ready position. As I watched the man who'd fathered me, I felt nothing but hatred. I loathed him and everything he stood for. Even in my debilitated state, my passion for him heated up.

I continued to watch the scene below. I couldn't understand what was being said because I couldn't hear. I tried to open my window, but in my weakened state, I was unable to do so. I was about ready to crawl back to my ragged blanket on the floor when I heard a lot of laughter and mockery. I heard a lot of derisive language and ridicule. About sixty men jeered, pointed, and taunted as a young woman was led, a rope around her neck, to the middle of the courtyard where she stood in front of my father.

I begged my body for strength. In my enfeebled state, my arms had become numb on the windowsill. It dawned on me that the young woman was on trial for something. My heart clutched as severe pain echoed through my body. A painful quiver moved up my spine. My heart feared for the young woman. I wanted to save her, to rescue her from these monsters more than anything else in the world. I figured they were trying the woman for being unfaithful. I heard the words for whore in three Arabic languages. The woman stood silently, never speaking a word. A black hood covered her head.

Finally, the jeering and heckling died down, and I heard my father pronounce the death sentence for the young woman. I watched mesmerized as the executioner pulled the black hood from the woman's face and exposed her to the crowd.

My heart stopped beating. I was paralyzed, but a weak, pitiful cry escaped from my throat. It was my mother who was being condemned to death. My soul cried. I was so helpless. My poor mother had never had a day of peace in her life since she met Faisal Muhammed on her twenty-second birthday, the day she'd fallen in love with the monster. The first day of the shattering of her life.

I was powerless as I watched the scene below me. I hoped my father would grant me one last visit with my mother. As I watched the men move and scatter, I glared at my father from the window. He knew I was there. Our eyes locked. I saw a sardonic, cynical look on his face. I was a healer, not a killer, but I'd never wished more for my Army-standard issue M9 mm weapon than I did now. If I had it, I'd blow his head off. Faisal continued to smile his derisive, satirical smile as I became weaker and weaker as I clung to the windowsill.

My strength waned. I pulled the rocking chair closer to balance my weight. I reached to steady myself on the wooden sill when I realized the men had returned. The terrorists had collected a large pile of stones and rubble.

My mind went crazy with realization, as I comprehended what was below me. Prisms and crystals erupted in my head. My mind was shredded by shards of glass. *They were going to stone my beautiful mother to death on my father's or-*

der. No. No. They couldn't. Her life had already been ruined by the monster below. No!

My mind went wild as I looked for something, anything to break the window and plead for her release. Finally, I reached as far as I could and grasped an old, hard-plastic Tiny Tears baby doll. I swung the doll against the glass as hard as I could and broke the window. I screamed at my father. "No. No! Don't you touch her!" My voice was a hysterical screech.

My father had broken me. I was begging, and I continued to beg.

He ignored me, and I watched the first five men cast stones at my mother's small, frail frame. The first two stones knocked her to the ground. The third stone hit her in the head.

I screamed again. "Let her go! Let her go!"

My father raised his hand to stop the stoning. A moment later, he left his chair. I knew he was coming for me, but that was okay if he'd let my mother live.

But I knew he wouldn't.

He was a monster.

Chapter 30

A few minutes later, I heard noise as several pairs of boots ran up the steps to my old playroom. Two men literally threw my mother's body at me. She whimpered as her body hit the floor and then remained quiet. I cursed them but pretended to be bound to my day bed. When they left, I rushed to my mother who was barely conscious. Her eyes were closed, and her blonde hair was matted with blood, dirt, and twigs.

I shook her gently. "Mother, mother. Are you okay?"

She didn't respond. I turned her head toward me. "Mother, Mom, it's me, Sonia. We're gonna be okay." Blood seeped from a gash on her lip where a stone had hit her. I raised her lip and examined her teeth. They seemed loose. I quickly assessed the rest of her body. Her shoulder was displaced and most likely broken. Bruises were beginning to form on her arms and legs. She had a huge contusion on her head. That worried me most of all. The thought of a head injury crossed my mind.

My mother remained unresponsive. I moved my body close and cradled her with my own. I slept briefly until her moans woke me.

I struggled to a sitting position. I looked down into her face. Her blue eyes were dark with fear and confusion.

"Mom. It's me. It's Sonia. You're in Syria. Faisal has us."

My mother moaned. Her eyelids closed. Her voice was faint. "What? Is that you, Sonia?"

"Yes, it's me, Mom." I hoped my voice didn't break. I wanted to be strong and take care of my mother. If I wasn't strong, I knew she would give up and will herself to die. I took a deep breath and continued. "We're going to be safe. Paul and Jeff will come and rescue us soon. I know they will."

My mother opened her eyes. They were a deep shade of blue. It was clear she recognized me. She reached for my hand. She stared at me for a moment.

I grasped her small hand. "We'll be out of here soon. Paul and his men will rescue us." I smiled down at her.

She shook her head slowly. "No, we won't, Sonia. No one is coming to get us. We're gonna die. Faisal will kill us. I always knew he would."

Chapter 31

It was predawn; four o'clock in the morning and the sky was pitch black. Twenty Delta Force operators jumped from three MH-60 Blackhawk Stealth helicopters. Their orders were to neutralize the enemy, free Sonia and her mother, and a capture/kill order for Emir Faisal Muhammed.

The long continuous curvature of the Blackhawks and lack of external riveting created shrouding around the helicopters and, although they could be seen from below, they looked like commercial airliners. Blackhawks evade radar and ground sensing equipment because of their design. The flat surfaces and sharp edges absorb radio waves and transfer them into heat which makes the craft almost invisible.

The twenty Halo operators jumped from a height of twelve thousand feet. Each operator wore a standard jump helmet, had an O2 tank on his back, and was dressed appropriately. The operators drifted through the air for six to seven seconds before their steerable parachutes opened. In less than two minutes, the operators were on the ground where they huddled for final plans and orders. Minutes later, using hand signals, they spread out to the bunkhouse, a twenty by sixty rectangular building expected to house multiple enemy combatants, Emir Faisal Muhammed's residence, and a storage barn.

Based on heat signature intelligence, generally seventy percent reliable, ten operators went to the bunkhouse. Five operators quietly moved to Faisal's primary residence. They entered, checked the first floor, and swiftly ran to the second floor where an estimated ten bodyguards slept. The guards were quickly neutralized. The final five Delta operatives headed toward the barn.

Three stun grenades were simultaneously tossed through bunkhouse windows. The flashbangs temporarily disoriented the terrorists sleeping in the building and allowed the Delta Force operators considerable advantage. The operatives aggressively entered through two doors and shot through several windows. Most of the sleeping terrorists were immediately killed. A firefight broke out, but within minutes, Delta Force exited the building. Not one terrorist remained alive.

Five American operators entered the Emir's residence. Using hand signals, they cleared the first floor and quickly climbed to the second floor where, once again, they used a flashbang grenade to stun and neutralize Faisal's bodyguards. Several minutes later, they were on the third floor of the residence where Faisal slept. The operators neutralized three additional bodyguards. They searched for the Emir. His bed, though slept in, was empty. Emir Faisal Muhammed wasn't there.

Two operators raced to the roof and saw Faisal at the far edge. Their plan to take the man alive was going south. The operatives sprinted toward him just as he jumped off the three-story roof. The two Americans stared at the ground. "His neck is broken," the first man said. "He's dead." The men quickly exited as the sound of nearby gunfire directed their attention to their comrades. They could see automatic weapons flare from the woods behind the Emir's house.

The first operator cursed under his breath. "What the hell is going on? Where's the gunfire coming from? We only know about three buildings."

The second operator shrugged. "Yeah. I don't know. Let's get the hell out of here. We need to recon with the others."

The other guy nodded. "Yeah, but we gotta check the body. Let's go down and take a closer look. For all we know, he's playing possum."

The first operator shook his head. "Nah. Forget the body... we gotta get out of here. We'll check him later."

The two men rushed down the three flights of steps, jumping over dead bodies on their way. They met up with the three operators on their team who were engaged in a firefight behind the residence with several unfriendlies who were camped in the woods. A few minutes later, the night was quiet.

Chapter 32

I awoke to the sound of stun grenades and automatic weapons fire. I reached out to touch my mother. I whispered in her ear in a soft voice. "They're here. They've come to rescue us. We're gonna be fine. It's Paul and his men. I can help you walk." I sat up and looked down at my mother who was barely alert. In fact, she was unresponsive. I shook her gently. "Mom, Mom, you've got to wake up. They'll be here in a few moments."

My mother didn't respond. I couldn't see her chest move. My heart fell, and my joy of rescue floundered. I put my ear to my mother's mouth and reached for her pulse. She was alive, but her pulse was weak and irregular. I knew she was close to death. A paralyzing pain passed through my heart as I looked at her.

"No, no. You can't die. We're gonna be rescued. Paul is here. And Jeff." I reached forward and pulled her up from the floor. She gasped, and her eyes shot open. She cried out in pain and fear. Her beautiful blue eyes were unfocused, and she seemed hysterical. I was frightened and didn't know what to do. I was afraid I'd scare her to death before our rescuers got to us.

I spoke softly. "Mom, it's me. Paul has come to rescue us. Can you move toward the door with me? I'll help you."

"All right, honey. I'll do my best." Melody's voice was weak and barely audible. Sonia looked into her eyes which were filled with confusion and doubt. She knew she'd have to help her mother move every inch of the way.

"Mom, we're gonna be fine. Paul's here with his men. We're going home."

My mother stared at me, her eyes unblinking. She obviously didn't understand. "Paul, who's Paul? Where are we, Sonia? What's all the noise? It sounds like fireworks." Then she laid back with exhaustion. The four short sentences had taken all her energy. I watched in horror as she faded away from me.

I panicked. My mother was incoherent. She was confused and barely conscious. "Momma, Paul, my Paul, is coming with his men to rescue us. We're going home."

"Paul's getting us out? Out of where?" Melody's eyes fluttered open as she tried to focus.

I could hardly look at my mother's battered face. One side of her head was swollen, and her eye was distorted. I briefly wondered again if the blows to her head from the stones had caused a concussion. The dim light of an old alarm clock showed darkened bruises on her arms and legs. Her shoulder was fractured and her arm hung by her side.

"That's good, honey," Melody murmured.

I could hardly hear her over the firefight outside. I touched my mother's forehead. She burned with fever. My heart froze. I couldn't... I wouldn't let my mother die when we were this close to freedom. "Mom, Mom, hang in there. They'll get us in a few minutes. Please." I held my mother's body as close to me as I could. I wanted my chilled skin to absorb the heat from her body. I hugged her as tightly as I could.

Melody seemed to understand. She nodded but remained unresponsive. She stared at me with her beautiful blue eyes, the same eyes that had captured the love of a Syrian monster almost forty years ago. The same eyes that had laughed and danced with me in the streets of Aleppo and on the ancient tiles of The Citadel. The eyes that welcomed me home to the United States at the age of eighteen after Faisal had abducted me. I locked eyes with her and talked softly as the minutes passed. I refused to let her die here like this at the monster's house.

The light drained from my mother's eyes. For a moment, I couldn't find her pulse, and I panicked. I cradled her body in my arms as she cried out in pain. *Good. At least she's still alive.* Even with all my years of medical training, I wasn't sure what to do. The bastards had broken her shoulder when they'd stoned her. Her head had been beaten with stones. I hoped they were dead, all of them, in the courtyard below. I hugged my mother tightly and prayed for rescue.

A second later, the door burst open and I heard something hit the floor. It was a stun grenade. A flashbang, a non-lethal sound bomb, designed to disable the enemy for a few moments. I wasn't the enemy, but, of course, they didn't know that. I'm sure my rescuers had no idea what they'd find in Faisal's barn. For a moment, I was blinded and confused. I was temporarily deafened by the blast. I couldn't see, or think.

Seconds later, four men in full battle armor, with assault rifles and night vision goggles, burst into the room. I heard the word "clear" and seconds later, two men were at our side. The room smelled of smoke and fire. I couldn't speak or see well, but relief flooded my mind, and my heart beat wildly in my chest. I gasped for breath. Tears flooded my eyes. The four men had American accents. They were American soldiers.

"Dr. Amon. Major Amon. Do you understand me? We are American soldiers. We're here to take y'all home. Both of you." The man was young and handsome. He had what appeared to be a short, blonde crew cut but I couldn't really say because of his helmet. He gave me a huge smile. His teeth were perfect.

"My father?" My body trembled with relief. "Where's my father?"

My rescuer's voice was matter-of-fact. "Not sure, ma'am. Either dead or captured. That I can assure you. No need to worry about him anymore."

My body shook with relief. I stared into the young man's green eyes which seemed greener from the glow from his goggles. I looked at his uniform. "You're more than American soldiers. You're Delta Force."

The man touched her hand. "First and foremost, we are American soldiers." He nodded toward Melody. "How's your mother?"

I shook her head. Tears flew into my eyes. "She's badly hurt. They stoned her this afternoon. Her shoulder is broken and possibly her hip. She may have a concussion." My voice faltered and then broke.

The young soldier took my hand in his. "We'll be gentle. We'll take care of her. And you, what are your injuries, Major?"

I didn't answer. "My father planned to stone her to death over three days. I heard him say that in the courtyard."

"That's not gonna happen, Major. I can assure you. We'll get you out of here in several minutes." His voice was strong, his tone gentle as he reassured me that we were safe.

I blinked back tears as I looked at my mother. She was unconscious, most likely from the pain. Then I looked up at my rescuer. "My father's a monster."

The soldier saw the terror in my eyes. He touched my arm and took my hand. He looked into my eyes. "Your father won't hurt anyone ever again, Major. And he certainly won't hurt you."

"He's dead?"

"We don't know. He'll be dead or captured." The operator nodded just as the first two men, presumably medics, reappeared with two stretchers and basic medical gear.

"We're taking you home, Major Amon, by way of Ramstein Air Force Base in Germany. We need to get both of you there ASAP." He smiled at me. "We'll take good care of both of you. Where are you hurt?"

I remembered he'd asked me that earlier. My thoughts returned to my body. My injuries. "My leg is broken, my shinbone, and I have a couple of broken ribs. The rest of me is just beaten up," I said, tears of gratitude in my eyes. When I wiped my eyes with my hand, I was surprised at the blood oozing from my face.

The medic nodded. "We'll move quickly. We've heard Faisal's men in Aleppo are on their way. Someone, probably one of the enemy combatants camped outside managed to get a message to them."

I watched as the four Delta Force operators carefully placed my tiny, fragile mother on the stretcher and started an IV. Their movements were swift and assured. They were tender and careful with her. She remained unconscious and didn't even flinch with the insertion of the needle. My heart hurt as I saw the bruises all over her body from the stones my father's hideous men had cast at her only hours earlier.

Then, it was my turn. I was stiff from inactivity, my movements delayed by the stun grenade. I accepted help from the Delta Force operators to get me on the stretcher. They secured my leg so I would be as pain-free as possible on my trip down the steps. They knew what they were doing.

Ten minutes later, my mother and I rested comfortably in a Blackhawk helicopter. Several minutes later, we were on our way to our destination where we would then be transferred to Ramstein Air Force Base in Germany. Then we'd be stabilized for transport to the United States. Then I'd be able to see my dog again. I missed her so much.

The entire predawn attack and destruction of my father's stronghold compound, the deaths of his closest men, and the obliteration of my childhood home had taken Delta Force operators less than twenty minutes. I learned later that they'd taken four prisoners.

When we were airborne, I touched the sleeve of an officer near me. "Can I talk to Colonel Paul Grayson? I was attached to him on this mission."

"Yes, of course, Major Amon. As a matter of fact, some of Colonel Grayson's men are currently engaged in a firefight with enemy combatants. He's at his base. Let me get a satellite phone and contact him for you."

I waited a moment as the soldier made the connection and handed me the phone.

"Sonia, Sonia, are you all right?" Paul's voice sounded funny. I guessed he was upset.

"Yeah, yes, I am. I'm okay," I murmured. "I've got a broken leg and a few ribs, maybe a black eye, but I'm okay."

I heard a huge sigh of relief. "I'm so glad. I was so worried. How about your mother? How's Melody?" Paul's voice was stronger now. I think he was just upset. And that was okay. After all, the man loved me.

I glanced over at my mother who seemed to be sleeping. "I think she's okay. She's really beat up, Paul." I took a deep breath. "Faisal had her stoned in the courtyard yesterday. About fifteen or twenty of his men had gathered and some of them threw stones at her, big stones." I gulped back a sob. I was gonna lose it, and I really didn't want to. I wanted to keep my composure in front of the brave young men who'd risked their lives to save us.

I heard what I think was Paul's fist hit the table. He was furious. I heard the intake of air that I knew so well. "He had her stoned? What a sick, cruel man."

"Yes," I wailed. "I think he's dead, but I'm not sure... I think they killed him." I paused and continued. "They said he was either dead or taken prisoner."

"I hope to hell he is," Paul blustered. "If he's not, I'll kill him myself with my bare hands." I knew that voice. I knew Paul would do just that. He'd kill my father. Somehow, that made me happy, and I felt even more loved. Or, perhaps I was just giddy from the pain medicine they'd stuck in my IV.

I laughed weakly. "I think someone has done that. Is Jeff there? I want to thank him."

"Yeah. He's right here." A second later, Jeff was on the line.

"Sonia, it's Jeff. Are you okay?" His voice was quiet, and he sounded concerned. I thought back over the times that Jeff had saved my tail. I was sure he was the one who'd gotten Delta Force in on the action.

"I'll live," I said as flippantly as I could. I smiled to myself. I knew Jeff Hansen had pulled every string he possibly could to save my life. Jeff was an incredible CIA operative with friends all over the world, and, at this point, his connections in Washington had saved my life and that of my mother. "When you get back to Washington, will you check on Tessa for me? I miss her so much."

"Of course, I will. I'll visit her and let her know you're doing fine," he assured me.

I sighed and took a deep breath. "Thank you, Jeff. Take her some bones, will you? And, I will be fine. I know I owe you my life." My voice was quiet. I was so thankful for my handler. "You've saved me so many times."

Jeff sighed and responded in his long-suffering voice, but I heard a smile in it. I could visualize him looking at me as he rolled his eyes. "Yeah, you do. Yeah, you do. So... from now on when I say 'no,' are you gonna listen?"

"Um, possibly not," I said glibly. "I guess it'll depend on the situation."

Jeff laughed. "You'll be fine. I'll catch up with you in Germany. Can you stay out of trouble until then?"

"Maybe, especially since I have a broken leg." I paused. "But I still thank you, Jeff. I love you. Thanks for saving my mother and me." I paused and added, "Don't forget about my dog!"

"I won't forget about Tessa. She's much better behaved than you are. But, you're welcome, but this is absolutely the last time, Sonia, and I mean it." I heard Jeff and Paul laugh and I laughed too. A moment later, Paul was back on the phone. His deep, calm voice comforted me.

"I love you, Sonia. Rest now, and I'll see you in Germany in a few days. I'll need someone to take command for me so I can come. Give your mother a hug."

"I love you too, Paul. I'll be there." I heard the satellite phone click off.

I closed my eyes and gave thanks for the United States of America and its Armed Forces. They'd offered me a safe place to live my torn and shattered life. My Army career had saved me from myself, and for that, I was grateful. Now, they'd saved me from my monster father, and for that, I was jubilant. Plus, they'd removed him from the face of the earth and I'd dearly loved hearing that.

The medic came over and put something else in my IV. I'm sure it was a pain reliever. I closed my eyes and slept until we touched down in Germany.

Six Weeks Later

Jeff and I sat in a small bistro just outside of Washington DC. It was our second lunch since my return from the Middle East. His smile was warm, and his eyes twinkled. Tessa lay at my feet.

"You're looking great, Sonia. No one would ever know you were beaten almost to death only a month ago." Jeff admired Sonia's shiny dark hair and dark eyes. She looked beautiful. "Not bad for an old, retired hard-assed Army Major."

I laughed. "Do I have to pay you for these compliments?"

"Sure, if you'd like," he teased.

I shook my head. "Well, I still know I was almost beaten to death, and I still feel the pain," I said as I pointed to the cane next to me and my plaster leg cast. Also, please don't make me laugh, because the ribs are still pretty painful and laughing really hurts!"

"I'll try to hold all jokes," Jeff promised. "How's your mother? Is she up and about?" His face was concerned. Melody's recovery had been slow and she remained traumatized from the experience.

I paused before I answered. "She's doing well. The whole thing, her being kidnapped, the stoning... well, she's doing the best she can. She's still pretty weak and thin."

"How about her mental health? Is she depressed?" Jeff's brow was furrowed.

I thought for a moment before I replied. "Well, she's kinda freaked out because her hair is falling out. Her doctor told her it was a reaction to the stress she'd been through. But, she's relieved that my father's dead." Sonia's heart lurched as a shadow passed across Jeff's face. *He is dead, isn't he?*

"It was a very successful mission. The captured hostile's confessions are invaluable and offer us good insight into ISIS's overall plan. Also, they gave us lots of information about funding, recruitment, and motivation. They were easy to crack, so everyone at the Agency and in the military was pleased."

A pain shot through my head and I was unable to respond for a few moments. The headaches and visual disturbances were continual since I'd returned to the U.S. "I'll tell you one thing, Delta Force is amazing. That attack seemed, at least from my perspective, to be totally synchronized. It seems like all three buildings were attacked at the same time. That required incredible planning." I hesitated for a moment, and then continued, "I owe them my life."

Jeff nodded. "Yeah. They're the cream of the cream and the best of the best. No question. It was perfectly orchestrated. Even the unforeseen, the attacks in the woods. It's amazing how well they can communicate with hand signals, and you're right, the flashbangs were synchronized. The mission was well planned and extraordinarily executed."

"I couldn't agree more." I picked up a potato chip and offered Tessa a piece of my sandwich. The chip was good. I still craved salt, although I knew I shouldn't have it based on the headaches I suffered. "By the way, why didn't they just bomb the bunkhouse?"

"They couldn't be sure there were no innocents in there. Plus, the heat signatures are only about seventy percent predictive. We just knew *somebody* was in there and we figured they weren't friendly but we couldn't be sure."

I nodded. I'd forgotten about the protection of innocents in war. "I'm fairly sure no one in that bunkhouse was an innocent."

Jeff nodded. "You're probably right. And, not to pat myself on the back, but I helped that happen." Jeff smiled at me with his eyes. He had a dreamy look in them.

"You did?" I goaded him. "Why am I not surprised? What did you do?"

Jeff reached for his iced tea. "Well, your buddy Sergeant Sneed and I took a hike around Faisal's compound and did a little recon. Then we worked with the Kurds, our best and possibly only ally in that area of the world. They have a stealth aircraft with the exhaust mounted on the top that reduces, if not prevents, the infrared signature so Faisal's boys couldn't pick us up from the ground."

"Wow, that's impressive, Jeff!" I kidded him. "I didn't know all of this stuff," I teased. Jeff had been an Army Ranger before he moved over to the CIA. He also had lots of friends in lots of powerful places.

Jeff rolled his eyes. "Anyway, that aerial surveillance picked up the heat signature and to a great extent, we knew exactly what Delta would walk into."

I was impressed and fortunate to have Jeff in my life. He'd saved my butt more than once. I reached for his hand. "I owe you my life, Jeff Hansen. You've kept me out of trouble for twenty years." My eyes filled with tears. "How can I ever thank you?"

I saw the red climb up Jeff's neck. I'd embarrassed him.

He laughed. "It'd make me happy if you stayed out of the Middle East and did all your doctoring and consulting at Walter Reed and the Army War College. That would make me so happy." Jeff winked and smiled.

I shook my head. "No can do, and you know that. I'm scheduled to return in a couple of months, just as soon as they let me out of physical therapy with my leg. Also, because of side effects from the flashbang, I have to see a psychiatrist." I made a face. I hated seeing a psychiatrist. It was a pain in my ass. The shrink assigned to me had deadpan, fish eyes and repeatedly asked me how things made me feel. He never cracked a smile.

Jeff's face was noncommittal. "What kind of symptoms are you having?" I figured Jeff already knew I had side effects from the stun grenade but wanted to hear it from me.

"Unpleasant ones," was my quick reply. I shook my head. "I get vivid flashes of light before my eyes, and I feel as though I'm momentarily blinded. Then my ears ring, and that's pretty horrible."

Jeff shook his head. "That sounds awful. It'll fade though."

"It is. My balance is affected, and I stumble around like a drunk. Sometimes I'm confused and can't remember things." I paused. My eyes filled with tears. "Honestly, Jeff. It's the most awful thing that's ever happened to me. I feel totally out of control as long as these attacks last."

Jeff rested his chin on his hand as he leaned forward. "How often do you have them?"

"Much too often. So far, two or three times a week. Sometimes every day! My psychiatrist thinks time will take care of them, but in the meantime – well, they don't even want me to drive, but I've fought that. The shrink thinks it could also be a manifestation of PTSD."

Jeff nodded. "Well, you've certainly been through enough to have PTSD. It's been less than two months. I'm sure it'll all come together," he assured me. His voice was soft, and I saw concern in his eyes.

I looked away. "Yeah. I suppose so. What's particularly bad is that I lose track of my thoughts and what I was doing for a few minutes." I smiled, but my smile was weak. "It's not good when your physician forgets what he or she is doing."

Jeff nodded. "Yeah. That's tough, but they're short-lived, so you get back on track quickly, right?"

I nodded. "Yeah. Pretty much, but it frightens me. Suppose I don't get better, and I can't practice medicine." I felt a couple of hot tears squeeze out of my eyes. The heat from the unshed tears made me dizzy for a moment. *Damn, I hope I don't have an attack here in front of Jeff.*

He took my hand. "You'll be fine – just give it time, Sonia. I promise you, I've seen this before."

"I hope so," I murmured in a small voice. The truth was I didn't know how quickly I'd recover, and I hadn't wanted to ask anyone.

Jeff nodded. He was concerned. This is exactly the information he'd received from Sonia's psychiatrist. The psychiatrist also mentioned he believed Sonia experienced delusions that accompanied the episodes, but she hadn't mentioned them.

"Let's take it slow and easy. I don't want you back in Syria – or anywhere for that matter - until you're a lot better." Jeff paused, "It's hard enough to keep up with you when you're healthy!"

It concerned him that she was scheduled to go back to Syria in eight weeks. "Unless you're a lot better, I can't recommend you return to the Middle East."

I quickly brushed his comment away and fed Tessa another bite of tuna. "Oh, I'll be fine in a few weeks. I'm sure they'll fade away. Besides, no one is gunning for me in Syria now. With my father dead..."

Jeff turned his head away from me, but I'd seen his face. I saw the flicker of uncertainty cross his face. My eyes locked with his. "My father is dead, right, Jeff?" Our eyes locked.

Jeff shrugged. "Faisal is as dead as he can be without a body."

I nodded as fear overtook my body. It crawled up my spine and rested in my heart. I couldn't breathe. I felt like I was suffocating. And a flash of light crippled my mind. I knew it. I'd felt it in my bones every day since I'd returned to the U.S. Faisal was still alive. The animal lived!

Jeff continued, "Without a body, we can't be absolutely sure." He glanced at me. I'm sure my eyes were wide with shock and fear. I hunched my shoulders and clasped my hands together to stop the trembling. My voice was shaky.

"Yes, but, Jeff, you said the Delta Force guys were sure he was dead." My voice was strained. "They thought his neck was broken from his jump from the roof. Right?" My heart pounded as I waited for Jeff's response.

"The operatives were positive. They were convinced his neck was broken. As you remember, Faisal jumped from a three-story building. But when all hell broke loose, there was no time to go back and check for signs of life." Jeff looked into my eyes and tried to convince me that things were okay. "But, as you know, when Colonel Grayson's men, specifically Sergeant Sneed's platoon, processed the scene at dawn, his body was gone." He paused. "They searched the perimeter for hours and never found a thing."

Sonia tossed her head. Her long coppery-brown hair shone in the sunlight from the Bistro window. "It's very possible his men carried him away for burial. He would have requested that."

Jeff nodded. "We're hopeful that's what happened." Jeff's fear, and increasingly a fear of his team, was that the body was a decoy and that Faisal hadn't even been staying in his residence that night. There was no possibility that he'd attempted suicide. That just wasn't done in the Muslim world. As time passed, Jeff and his team were more and more convinced that Emir Faisal Muhammed was still alive. But he had no proof.

I shook my head. I couldn't believe it. Was it possible that Faisal survived a broken neck? "I can't believe this. Have you heard anything indicating that he's alive?"

Jeff avoided my eyes. "Unfortunately, I have. One of my contacts told me there was a rumor that the Emir survived, somehow got medical attention, and was in Aleppo." He saw me clasp my arms to my body. I'd turned to ice. My body shook, and a shot of light crippled my mind. Tessa stood and nuzzled her nose to my hand. She'd picked up on my change of mood. My hands trembled. For a moment, I rocked from side to side but quickly recovered. *Was I having a seizure? What was wrong with me?* Uncertainty clouded my judgment. I was an imbecile. A crazy lady. A psych patient.

Jeff watched me with concern on his face. He laid his arms on the table, palms up.

I found my voice. "Oh, I hope you're wrong. But regardless, please don't tell my mother. She'll never have any peace of mind if she thinks he's still alive."

Jeff nodded. "I promise. In fact, I'm not convinced he's alive. As I said, my contact said he'd only heard rumors. We still hear two or three time a year that Elvis is alive."

I grinned. "That's true. And, he's all over Vegas."

Jeff nodded. "There are no actual sightings of Faisal by villagers or informants or proof that he's alive." Jeff gave me a hard look. "But until we have proof, we have to assume there's a possibility."

I nodded. My breath came more easily. My mind only heard the word "possibility." Perhaps my monster father was dead. That's what I prefer to think. My body relaxed. "Promise to keep me in the loop about this, Jeff." I requested as a text sounded on both our phones.

"I promise," Jeff said as he picked up his phone. I reached for mine at the same time.

I read the message. My vision clouded and I was dizzy. I looked at the text again. It was three short sentences.

Colonel Paul Grayson critically injured by sniper fire outside of Aleppo. Airlifted to Germany. Condition: Critical.

Jeff and I stared at each other. I spoke. "Sniper fire? Why would he be hunted by a sniper?"

Jeff shook his head. "I've no idea, but I'm headed to Germany. I'm going to Ramstein to check this out, then to Paul's garrison."

"I want to go," I insisted. "I must go to Paul. Please, will you arrange it?"

Jeff didn't respond at first. He looked at me and my injuries.

"Please Jeff. I won't hold you back, I promise." My voice sounded desperate.

Jeff considered my request. "I will. Let's get out of here, Sonia. Pack a bag. We'll probably leave around midnight." Jeff immediately knew his judgment was poor and flawed. Sonia had no business outside of the United States.

I stood and stared at the half of my tuna fish sandwich that remained. I'd been so excited about lunch with Jeff. I'd felt well an hour ago and now... well, I was frightened, terrified, and panicked. Plus, Paul, the love of my life, my husband to be, was possibly dying in a helicopter.

My body was wooden as I rose from the table. My broken leg would hardly move. I reached for my cane and handed Tessa the rest of my sandwich. She wolfed it down in one gulp. We left the restaurant.

Jeff assisted me to my SUV.

"Are you okay to drive? If not, I can drive you and wait for you to pack. Otherwise, I'll pick you up at eleven at your place."

"I'll be fine," I assured him. "This is just a shock, but I'll be fine. I'm going home, pack, and check with my office. I'll have to let Frances know my plans. I'll see you later," I promised.

Jeff nodded and gave me a kiss on the cheek. "Be safe, Sonia."

I drove the short distance back to my house. My mind was tired. Overwhelmed with the possibilities. *Who had tried to assassinate Paul Grayson?* Terrorists owned sniper rifles and used them, but Paul was hardly known to the locals, but still, as a military commander in the United States Army, he'd be a target. Particularly a military commander in the middle of an ISIS stronghold. My heart sank deep into my chest, so deep I could hardly breathe. I reviewed the situation in my mind. *Who would assassinate Paul?*

I knew.

Unless he was truly dead, my father would. If he wasn't dead, I was sure he'd tried to assassinate the man that I loved. That's something the monster would do.

I didn't know, but I had a feeling I'd know soon. I accepted this fact calmly.

I limped upstairs and pulled my small Army issued suitcase from my closet. I prepared for my trip to Germany. Until I was paralyzed by flashing lights and confusion. *Damn that flashbang.*

I staggered to a chair in my bedroom. Tessa watched me with sad eyes. She knew I was leaving. I seemed to break her heart every time I left.

But one day that would change.

~ The End ~
But this is not the end....

Please enjoy a sample of the next book in this chilling new series:
Delusion Proof (Book 2)

Prologue

I'm only aware of fear.

It's so all-consuming that every element of my body is screaming for relief. The muscles want to relax, the heart to slow, my lungs to pull in unsullied air and the blood to return to those paths that keep me alive.

It's my brain that won't relinquish its call to battle and yet can't identify the danger. What is this hell? It's mine and mine alone. It's what makes my days calm and rational by contrast and yet the exhaustion permanently intrudes.

It's behind me. No! It's at my side. No! I risk a backward glance at my pursuer, but he's hidden in the fog. I know it's male; it always has been. It's imperative I escape, not just for myself, but for the others he hunts.

I can do it again, just as I've done it before. I take three long strides with what energy remains and then up! I leap up and take flight. I fight the air beneath my feet as a swimmer attempts to outswim the shark, she knows is tracking her. Am I high enough? Am I out of reach?

I need to hide, to blend in with something obscure so I'm not recognized. A bush? In the crevasse of a rock? My body is flexible and if I can just get far enough ahead, around a bend so it cannot track me.

There! A tree with centuries of age. Its branches bear large, flesh-colored fruits. I push against the air in one last lunge and aim for a thick limb. Success! I wind myself around the limb and brace so I can go forever without movement. My mind goes into hibernation and with that, I am invisible.

The swirl of blackness pauses beneath my tree, and I hear its breath; heaving and moist with the mucus of overly-strained lungs. I cannot pray or else I again become visible, so I watch... and wait.

I hear it draw in a breath of determination, and as I watch, it spins forward, fire and the smell of death in its wake. Soon, it has pursued the wrong path, and I am safe. For now. Until tomorrow... when I must come up with yet another strategy to escape him and survive.

My nausea wakes me, and I'm drenched with perspiration. This wasn't new; in fact, it's very, very familiar and I knew just how long it would be before I re-acclimated to my surroundings and felt safe again. I put my mind through its paces.

The specter that followed could only have been the branches sweeping my window in the rising wind. The black swirls were the fractures of light from the street lamp at the curb below. The fear was because that's how I've survived. The tree with heavy fruits was my strategy to live just one more day. The scent of death always follows me; it doesn't frighten me. Indeed, it brings with it a sense of failure. Someone I could not get to in time; someone I loved but could not help and perhaps someone whose love I would never have but forever try to rationalize its absence.

I rose from the trampled sheets and heard the familiar floor creaks, guiding me to the bathroom, although I refused to open my eyes. Turning the brushed nickel faucet that I'd so lovingly picked out, I let the water resume its cold and then spooned handfuls over my face.

Sanity returned and with it the relief that the rest of the night was mine to recover. I *would* forget, I swore again. I would forget... and one day I would be free of him.

Chapter 1

The transport plane touched down on the tarmac in Ramstein, Germany with injured aboard. Although still weak and incapacitated by a broken leg, I hadn't come for treatment, but to tend to Paul. My fiancé was barely hanging on, the target of sniper fire in Aleppo. The only question that remained, beyond that of whether he could survive, was who had ordered him attacked?

As astounding as it might seem, there could be only one answer; one person who would try to kill the man who was closest to my heart. My dead father, Faisal.

That summoned the second, and perhaps the most lethal question of all. Was my father truly dead? Had he managed to outwit American soldiers in a staged leap from a third-story roof, only to have somehow disappeared when they came to inspect his body?

For me, Sonia Amon, the first question held the spirit and security of my heart, but the second held more hatred than I'd thought myself capable of feeling. The Emir, the icon of terror and horror who had continually haunted my life, was still most likely at work. No matter who heard your prayers, it seemed, evil never dies.

Despite my own injuries from being cruelly and sadistically beaten by my father's own men at his order, I struggled to walk off the plane and climb into the vehicle Jeff had waiting for our transport to the nearby Landstuhl Regional Medical Center or LRMC. As we approached the modern façade of the hospital with its curved central structure, fortified by an ultra-modern, unadorned wing, waves of recognition returned. I'd been there before, too many times. LRMC has a wholly unsavory reputation as being one of the largest sources of donor organs in the European region. Mutilated bodies with no hope rolled in one door, and recipients' lives rolled out another. It was a factor of war, not of pride.

I was asked for my credentials and handed them over.

"You're retired, Dr. Amon."

"Yes, I am."

"I'm sorry, ma'am, but only military personnel with clearance are permitted past this point."

I looked at Jeff and then back at the young guard with the fresh face and unblemished air of self-importance. I bit back something sarcastic and instead decided to appeal to something more important. "He's my fiancé. I'm also his personal physician, flown in from the States."

The young guard seemed thrown by this; it was a combination of credentials he'd never been presented with before. Jeff also sensed his indecision and motioned me with a nod of his head to step back. His head bent, he told the guard in very few, but potent, connected words that seemed to change the guard's point of view and he nodded and motioned me past.

I was unwilling to be in a wheelchair. It was not a place for weakness; but to be brave no matter the cost. I leaned on Jeff's arm but tried to keep it casual if others looked. He escorted me down two halls with railings affixed to the walls. I eyed them with desire but kept going. The further we went, the fewer smiles we saw. The nurses' stations became collections of monitors, and no one was exchanging pictures their children had drawn. These were the halls where soldiers came to live or die; most of them unaware their life was at that point.

Jeff came to a halt before a room with glass walls—various stickers of warning affixed to the door frame. I knew the routine, but it still hit hard when the dangers represented involved someone you love.

Then I saw him, surrounded by monitors that beeped, charting his heart rate and aiding his brain in what it currently could not do on its own. Paul couldn't breathe. A huge monster of a machine did that for him. That grieved my heart. His head was swathed in white bandages; his eyes closed and motionless. I knew without talking to his doctors that he had a severe head injury; any head injury is serious. The question lay in what he could do and who he would be if he awakened.

I reached out and touched the back of his hand, careful not to disturb the IV inserted there. Tears pooled in my eyes. Those were *my* hands; they caressed my skin and held me tight when the nightmares came. I could feel the tendons and strength, but now the surface was dry and thin-looking with bruises colored red, purple and blue. It broke my heart. There was absolutely nothing I could do but be there. I couldn't reach him now and that grieved my heart.

"Oh, Paul... I'm here. I hope you can hear me. I'm here for you. It's Sonia, Paul. You'll be fine. You just rest now; you're in good hands." My words choked in my throat. I stifled a cough. He *was* in good hands, as I had always been with him.

"Jeff, I want to stay." My eyes beseeched him.

Jeff shook his head. "Sonia, you need to rest. The flight, the stress, your leg. Why don't you let me get us someplace to stay, and you rest for a few hours? He'll be here."

I looked up at Jeff, my dark eyes hungry for encouragement. "You think so? I know you're not a medical professional, but do you really think so?"

He hesitated the briefest second and then said, "I've seen men in far worse shape pull through." A clever answer. Jeff was good at clever answers. After all, he was CIA.

I heard the warning in his voice. I couldn't shake the subtle fear that Jeff had brought me all this way because no one believed Paul would survive. I was, in short, saying my goodbyes. I didn't give speech to the fear. To do so was to change the fates of possibilities. I leaned over and kissed Paul's forehead and then nodded to Jeff, and we ambled back down the hallway and out into the night air.

"Why would anyone do that to another human just because he could?" I voiced my anger and resentment, and both of us knew who we suspected. But there was no proof—at least not yet. I couldn't talk about this with anyone but Jeff. Not my mother; she was the last person. It would be like whiplashes to make her relive the torture they administered to her. She still had excruciating headaches from the stoning my father had inflicted on her petite body. At least I was younger, taller, and stronger. My bones had given, but my spirit would not.

I could have talked to Paul, but for now, he was sleeping to hold on to the thread of life within him. I would have to deal with it myself. At least, I would try.

Dear reader,

Thank you so much for reading ***Shatter Proof***[1], the first book in the **Sonia Amon Medical Thriller Series**. I hope you enjoyed it. Since reviews are very important to Indie authors, if you did enjoy this I would be delighted if you would be so kind as to leave a review.

I always want to hear from and connect with my readers. Please feel free to contact me at any time with questions, ideas for new books, or just plain anything. I am happy to answer any questions. Visit my website to see more of my books and join my newsletter at www.judithlucci.com[2] .

Feel free to email me at judithlucciwrites@gmail.com anytime!

Once again, many thanks for reading my book!

Judith

You can find me on social media too!

BookBub[3] | Facebook[4] | Twitter[5]

---

1. *https://www.amazon.com/dp/B07XQJF8JT*

2. http://www.judithlucci.com

3. https://www.bookbub.com/authors/judith-lucci

4. https://www.facebook.com/groups/1238961029502128/

5. https://twitter.com/JudithLucci